2008

Traci Douglass is a *USA TODAY* bestselling author of contemporary and paranormal romance. Her stories feature sizzling heroes full of dark humour, quick wit and major attitude, and heroines who are smart, tenacious and always give as good as they get. She holds an MFA in Writing Popular Fiction from Seton Hill University, and she loves animals, chocolate, coffee, hot British actors and sarcasm— not necessarily in that order.

Also by Traci Douglass

One Night with the Army Doc
Finding Her Forever Family

Discover more at millsandboon.co.uk.

A MISTLETOE KISS FOR THE SINGLE DAD

TRACI DOUGLASS

MILLS & BOON

Published in Great Britain 2019
by Mills & Boon, an imprint of HarperCollins*Publishers*
1 London Bridge Street, London, SE1 9GF

© 2019 Traci Douglass

ISBN: 978-0-263-08095-7

MIX
Paper from
responsible sources
FSC™ C007454

This book is produced from independently certified FSC™ paper
to ensure responsible forest management.
For more information visit www.harpercollins.co.uk/green.

Printed and bound in Great Britain
by CPI Group (UK) Ltd, Croydon, CR0 4YY

To my family, and to all those lovely summers
we spent together on the beaches of Pentwater...

CHAPTER ONE

"I'M SORRY. COULD you repeat that, please?" Dr. Christabelle Watson blinked at the rather uncomfortable-looking lawyer sitting across the desk from her. "I don't think I heard you correctly."

Dylan Carter, the only attorney in tiny Bayside, Michigan, and therefore the person handling her aunt Marlene's estate, took a deep breath. "Um…okay. Sure. It says here your aunt left half of her practice to you and the other half to Dr. Nicholas Marlowe."

Nick, who sat next to her, shifted in his seat and straightened the dark jacket of his suit. Once he'd been a pediatric surgeon in Atlanta. Now he was back in their hometown as well, working as a GP.

Her aunt Marlene had been a general practitioner as well, a pillar of the Bayside community, liked and respected by all. Seemed everyone had turned out for her aunt's funeral earlier in the day and said their fond farewells and given condolences to Belle on her loss.

A loss that had been made even harder because she'd had no idea her aunt's cancer had progressed to stage four—terminal. Her chest ached anew with sorrow and regret. If only she'd known her aunt was so sick.

If only…

She tried to console herself with the fact that even

if she had known the severity of her beloved aunt's illness, it wasn't like she could have easily flown home to Michigan anyway. Not with a packed list of new patient consults back in California and a practice partnership on the line. Aunt Marlene wouldn't have wanted that anyway. She'd hated being fussed over, especially when she didn't feel well.

Belle sniffled and twisted a tissue in her hands. Everything was such a mess.

Life had certainly taken a strange turn in the past twenty-four hours. Yesterday her boss, Dr. Reyes, had wanted to meet with her about the partnership right before she'd received the call about her aunt. Now the world as she knew it had changed forever. She'd filled out the required bereavement paperwork with Human Resources, made her quick excuses to Dr. Reyes, then rushed to catch a red-eye flight to Lansing.

Everything after that was a bit of a hazy blur.

She cleared her constricted throat and forced herself to focus on the attorney once more. "There must be some mistake."

"Nope. No mistake." Dylan frowned at his copy of her aunt's will and pointed at a few particular lines. "Right here. See?"

He held the document toward her so she could look for herself.

She squinted down at the legalese. Yep. Right there in black and white.

All assets divided equally between Christabelle Watson and Nicholas Marlowe.

Nick too took the opportunity to lean in and Belle sat back fast, keeping as much distance between them as possible. His scent—soap and fabric softener—was the same as she remembered. His warmth penetrated the sleeve of her black blazer, sending tingles of unwanted awareness through her. Darn him. Even after everything he'd put her through, she still had the same tingling reaction whenever he was around. Not that she'd let him know.

Nope. Where Nicholas Marlowe was concerned, Belle had built her barriers high and strong.

Still, bone-deep exhaustion and grief threatened to overwhelm her, and she blinked hard against the sting of unshed tears. As a physician, she'd learned to mask her emotions behind a thick layer of professional stoicism— a necessity when personal feelings could lead to disaster with a patient. There were some who said she'd gotten too good at it, though, like with the few men she'd dated over the years. But at times like these it was the only thing that kept her going.

She clasped her hands in her lap to hide the slight tremble in her fingers and ignored the vibrating cell phone in her pocket. "Can you at least tell me how long it might take to get this all settled, Dylan? I have pressing matters back in California. Consultations and patients and—"

"Shouldn't your aunt's last wishes take precedence here?" Nick asked, his tone cold. His voice held a raw edge she didn't recall from their high-school days together. Gone were his easy smiles and easy banter. Then again, they were different people now. After graduation, she'd gone off to UCLA, then a surgical fellowship at Harvard. Nick had graduated at the top of his class from the University of Michigan, then done medical school at Northwestern. He'd also gotten married before he'd finished his residency, the very thing he'd told Belle he'd never do.

She gave an ironic snort. He'd broken up with her in

senior year, saying they were too young and being tied down would only hold her back. Then he'd turned right around and married someone else a few years later. Of course, it didn't help she'd found out by accident either. God, what a naive fool she'd been back then. She'd shown up at his apartment complex in Evanston, Illinois, hoping to talk to him about the career choice looming on her horizon. After all, she and Nick had been friends since childhood, despite their painful breakup. No one had ever known her better or understood her more. So she'd made a rash decision and shown up at his place, only to find a celebration in full swing in the common area of his building. An engagement party for Nick and the woman he was going to marry. A woman who'd also been obviously pregnant with his baby.

Even all these years later, those memories sliced deep.

Hurt and embarrassed, she'd left without ever speaking to Nick.

Belle had still loved him then, but he'd moved on. Moved on and left her behind, shattering her hopes they might one day reconcile and get back together. Now she'd put her work and her professional life first, only dating men who weren't interested in anything long term, keeping her heart and her emotions out of the equation.

She glanced over toward the corner where an eight-year-old boy played on a tablet. No denying Connor was Nick's son. Same curly brown hair and adorable dimples as his father.

Belle hazarded another look at Nick, the man who'd once been her whole world. With dark shadows marring the skin beneath his eyes and a shadow of stubble on his jaw, he looked as weary as she felt.

Aunt Marlene had mentioned his wife had passed away two years previously. Being a single parent wasn't easy and Belle couldn't imagine how hard it must've been for Nick to deal with the loss of a spouse plus raising his son alone. And poor Connor. Belle had lost her own parents at the same age Connor was now. It had been devastating. If Aunt Marlene hadn't taken her in and given her a loving, stable home, God only knew where she might've ended up.

Nick caught Belle's gaze, his expression wary. Years earlier, his soulful brown eyes had sparkled with mirth, ready for any challenge, always up for anything...

Now they stared at her, flat and somber.

"You said there was a stipulation?" Nick asked, refocusing his attention on the attorney.

"Right. Yes," Dylan said. "Marlene wants you both to reopen the free clinic one last time before you settle the estate."

"What?" Belle sat back, shocked. She only had three days of bereavement leave. "The free clinic isn't held until Christmas Eve."

"Dad?" Connor said from the corner. "I'm hungry."

"We'll eat in a minute." Nick frowned at Dylan. "That's nine days from now."

Belle rubbed her forehead. "I'm sorry. I want to respect my aunt's wishes, but I've got obligations in Beverly Hills. I can't drop everything. There has to be a way around it. Perhaps we could hold the clinic sooner?"

"That's impossible." Nick scrubbed a hand over his face and gave an aggrieved sigh. "It'll take a week or more just to get everything ready and I'm sure there are repairs to be made. The clinic was pretty run-down the last time I was there. Besides, I have my own practice to contend with before the holidays."

"Sorry, guys," Dylan said. "But Marlene had this will drafted through an estate lawyer in Lansing last year and it's airtight. I've checked. Honestly, the fastest way to get all of this settled is to honor your aunt's final wishes and reopen the free clinic on Christmas Eve."

Frustrated, Belle finally gave in and pulled out her cell phone, to find a text from Dr. Reyes shown on-screen.

Why aren't you answering my calls?

Irritated, Belle clicked off the device and slid it back into her pocket, heat prickling her cheeks. In the operating room she was famous for her cool, calm demeanor under pressure, but spending five minutes with Nick beside her again—bringing up memories of the past— had her cage thoroughly rattled. Belle didn't like it. Not to mention the free clinic was what had brought her and Nick together in the first place, helping out Aunt Marlene, working side by side to clean exam rooms or prep patients or wrap instruments for sterilization. It was because of those days that the smell of antiseptic still made her smile…

Ugh. Belle shook off those memories and turned to Nick. "I'm trying to be practical here. I'd think you'd appreciate my efforts, considering your busy work schedule and your son. I loved my aunt. I'd do anything for her, but—"

"Except honor her final wishes."

"How dare you?" Outrage stormed through Belle like a thundercloud. She sat back and crossed her arms. "Dylan, are we finished? I'd like to get a good night's sleep and consider this all again with a clear head in the morning. Can we continue this tomorrow?"

"Not so fast," Nick answered instead, pinching the bridge of his nose between his thumb and forefinger. "I'll need to check my schedule to see if I can fit in another meeting. My clinic is slammed this time of year as it is, and I need to check with my physician's assistant to be sure she can handle the extra workload. Plus, Connor needs to be picked up from school. Then there's dinner and getting him to bed." At Belle's irritated sigh, he narrowed his gaze on her. "Or maybe you'd prefer I pull an all-nighter like I did in college?"

She hid her cringe admirably. Any reminder of college and that awful night she'd made her surprise visit to see him had the knots of tension in Belle's upper back quadrupling.

"Dad." Connor's tone grew more plaintive. "I'm starving."

"Give me one more minute." Nick gave a long-suffering sigh, his voice dull. "Look, I realize I'm the last person you want to partner with here, Belle, but Marlene made it clear in her will this is what she wanted and unless we do this together, it will never work."

Darn it, he was right. Much as she hated to admit it.

Fatigue and sadness crowded in around her once more, but duty compelled her to stand firm. "I want to help, I do. But my boss is already texting me about his unreturned calls." She shook her head. Disappointing people was her least favorite thing, even people like Nick. "Plus, I've got opportunities on the line back in California. I have to keep my priorities straight."

"What about your aunt's wishes?" Nick said. "Shouldn't *she* be your priority right now?"

The words struck her like a slap in the face and ricocheted inside her chest like shrapnel. When she'd been eighteen she would've given anything to hear him ask her to stay. Now it felt like one more complication in an already chaotic mess.

Her cell phone buzzed again, most likely with another text from Dr. Reyes.

Through the window behind Dylan's desk the sky glowed pink and gold and deepest purple as the sun set and people milled about outside after the funeral. Belle smoothed her hand down her black skirt, her head aching. She'd only returned to Bayside to close this chapter of her life for good. With Aunt Marlene gone, there was no reason for her to come back here again after this. She was alone in the world now and the thought made her weary beyond her thirty-six years.

"Don't mean to rush you, folks." Dylan cleared his throat. "But I've got a holiday dance recital for my daughter tonight, so if we could wrap this up, I'd really appreciate it."

"Right." Determined, Belle stood and grabbed her bright red cashmere coat from the back of her chair. "I guess that's it, then."

"Oh, there is one more thing." Dylan pulled something out of one of his desk drawers. "Marlene had a small amount left in her savings after the medical bills were paid. It goes to each of you." He passed two envelopes across the desk. "Ten thousand dollars each. And there's a copy of the will in there for each of you too."

Belle tucked the envelope inside her handbag without looking at it. "Nick, if you can't make a formal meeting, perhaps we can schedule a conference call tomorrow to discuss this further?"

He shook his head. "I'll make it work. Your aunt wanted us to do this and I intend to honor her final wishes."

A swirling vortex of grief opened in the pit of Belle's stomach, making her temples throb.

"Dad," Connor said, frowning. "I'm hungry-y-y…"

Nick waved his son over then walked to the door before turning back to Belle. "Do you have plans for dinner? If not, you're welcome to join us at Pat's. We can talk more there."

Honestly, she didn't have plans. In fact, her stomach was rumbling, and her new designer pumps were pinching her toes something terrible. She'd also not had a chance to pick up any groceries and nothing stayed open past eight in Bayside. "Fine. But only to discuss the clinic, not to socialize."

"Agreed." Nick pulled on his own black wool coat then ushered her and his son outside. "No socializing here. Promise."

As they headed into the chilly mid-December night, Nick eyed Belle's stiletto pumps with trepidation. Seemed she'd forgotten what winters could be like here in Michigan. Sure enough, as they trudged across the slick pavement, her feet slipped, and she clutched his arm like a lifeline.

"You need boots."

"I have boots. They're in my suitcase inside the funeral home." She stiffened beside him and released his arm, clutching her coat tighter around herself. "I'll be sure to wear them tomorrow."

He shook his head. Her coat probably cost more than his house and all its contents. When he'd been at the top of the pediatric surgery ladder in Atlanta, he'd seen plenty of women dressed to the nines in designer duds. Hell, he'd worn his share of tuxes back then too. Now, though, he dressed for comfort. He'd moved back to Bayside a year and a half ago, given up his high-pressure lifestyle and all the stress along with it, and wouldn't change his decision for the world. Connor was better off with fresh air and room to grow. Losing his wife, Vicki, had been hard on both of them, but Bayside was home.

Always had been. Always would be. At least for him.

He hunched farther down inside his wool coat and turned the collar up against the brisk wind now rolling in off Lake Michigan. Weathermen predicted snow tonight, from what he'd heard on the radio on his way over to the funeral.

Belle slipped again. He reached for her elbow, but she pulled away. "I've got it."

"Yeah. I can see that."

He stifled a grin at her peeved glare.

Connor walked along ahead of them, oblivious.

"Don't cross the street by yourself, son," Nick called. "Wait for us."

Belle gave him some serious side-eye at the same time his son gave him a perturbed stare.

"He's eight, right?" she asked.

"Yes." Nick bristled at her judgmental tone. Fine. Maybe Connor was old enough to start doing things on his own, but Nick wasn't there yet. He was trying, but his son was growing up—far faster than Nick wanted sometimes—and guilt lingered in his heart. He did his best to be both mom and dad to Connor, but there were only so many hours in a day and it was just the two of them. Besides, Belle had no right to question his parenting style. Still, in an effort to keep the peace he swallowed the words he wanted to say and instead pointed to a redbrick building across the street on the corner. "Diner's over there."

"I know where Pat's is." Belle's tone snapped with

affront. So much for not arguing. "I'm from here, re-member?"

"Figured you forgot. Kind of like your boots."

She glared at him, her green eyes glittering in the dim streetlight.

The three of them crossed the street and pushed inside the restaurant. Pat Randall—the diner's proud owner for over thirty years—waved to Nick from behind the counter, oblivious to the tension pulsating around them like a force field. "Hey, Doc. Con."

A few other patrons were eating a late dinner there too, probably having wandered over after Marlene's service. Some were his patients, like little Analia Hernandez and her family. She was the same age as Connor and would've been in his class at school, but she'd been born with Crouzon syndrome, a rare genetic condition that had caused the bones of her skull to fuse prematurely. There was no mental deficiency associated with the disorder, thank goodness, but the concave shape of her midface did contribute to the little girl's breathing issues. Still, Analia was happy and confident, always quick with a grin and brimming with curiosity. Analia raised a hand at Connor as they passed their table. "Hey, Con."

"Hey, Ana." Con waved back.

They took a table near the far wall and Belle sat gingerly, like the whole place might blow up in her face. Nick sat in the chair beside Connor's, across from Belle, and raked a hand through his hair, his appetite buried under the uncomfortable feelings stirred by seeing Belle again after all these years. With her living out in California, it had been easier for him to keep her as more of an abstract notion in his head.

A woman, *the* woman, from his past. Always there,

but quarantined, like a dangerous virus that could easily hijack his system. Now, though, with her back in Bayside, even temporarily, he was forced to reconcile the promise he'd made to Vicki with reality. He'd let Belle go back in high school and obviously she'd moved on and done well for herself. She'd left Bayside and him behind eighteen years ago and hadn't looked back since. He should be happy, overjoyed, well and truly done with it all.

Why then did his heart pinch a little each time he caught sight of Belle now?

Must be stress. Had to be. He'd headed to Marlene's funeral directly after spending sixteen hours in his clinic and he had another full schedule tomorrow. Maybe Belle had been correct. Maybe they should have put this conversation off until he'd gotten some sleep, had some peace and quiet to get his life in order again.

Except deep down he knew it wouldn't change anything.

Work. Connor. Home.

Those were his driving forces now.

The only things that mattered.

Dinner with Belle, anything to do with Belle really, shouldn't be on his radar.

Other than reopening the free clinic one last time. He owed that to Marlene, even if it would be about as much fun as a root canal.

"What can I get you folks to drink?" Pat asked, setting three glasses of water on the table.

Belle perused her choices, frowning. "Do you have anything organic?"

"Uh…we've got tea."

"Is it green?"

"Brown, last time I checked." Pat chuckled. "Unless it's gone bad."

"I'll stick with water, thank you," Belle said, her expression dour.

"Sure thing." Pat jotted something on his little pad, then grinned. "So great to see you again, Belle. I'm so sorry about what happened to Marlene."

"Thank you, Mr. Randall."

"Please, call me Pat. We're like family around here."

She nodded, then went back to looking at her menu.

Nick cleared his throat. "Con and I will have sodas, Pat."

"Cherry flavor in those?"

"Of course." Nick winked at his son.

"Be right back." Pat walked away, leaving them alone again.

Even beneath the diner's fluorescent lights, Belle's auburn hair still glowed like wildfire. A trait she and her aunt had shared. Her mom too, if Nick remembered right. Of course, he'd only been eight too when her parents had died in a car accident. The whole town had turned out for their funeral, as well. He pictured little Belle back then, sitting alone on Marlene's porch, not crying, not scared, just sort of oddly stoic.

Kind of like she was now.

Belle leaned closer to him, close enough for him to catch a hint of scent—something fresh and floral with a hint of mint. "You don't let him order his own food either? How controlling of you."

"Remind me again when you became a parenting expert?" He clasped his hands on the table, all traces of tenderness toward Belle vanishing. Connor's well-being was his top priority in life. Period. Amen. He'd promised Vicki he'd take care of their son and he intended to keep that vow. He changed subjects to safer territory. "How's California?"

"Sunny." Her phone continued buzzing like an angry bee.

"Can't you just turn that thing off while we eat?" he asked her. "Don't you have an answering service to field calls when you're out of the office?"

"Yes." Her green eyes flashed again with annoyance. "My boss is trying to reach me."

"Here we are, folks." Pat returned with their drinks. "What are we having for dinner?"

"Connor and I will split a burger and fries. Cheese, no onion. Medium-well."

"Great." Pat wrote down his order. "And for you, Belle?"

"I'll have the house salad. No cheese or croutons. Dressing on the side. Fat-free Italian. Hold the bread stick too."

"Or you could just bring her a cardboard box, Pat. It'll be just as tasty," Nick said.

The two men chuckled, and she gave them an impassive stare.

"While I always appreciate your culinary opinions, Nick, I'll stick with what's healthy." She jammed her menu back into the holder and gave Pat a cool smile. "And could I have a lemon wedge for my water? Thank you."

Pat left, shaking his head.

"Are your parents still in town?" Belle asked as she unbelted her expensive coat to reveal the equally expensive tailored suit beneath, all sharp lines and jagged edges. So different from the cute, geeky girl he'd fallen in love with back in high school. Gone were her soft heart and pretty curves, her lilting giggles as they'd dreamed about taking the medical world by storm, like all those TV doctors on their favorite shows.

Nope. Not going there.

He shoved away the pang of nostalgia welling inside him for the kids they'd once been—so young, so idealistic, so naive—and took a deep breath. The air filled with the smell of grease and the sizzle of frying meat.

What had happened between them in the past didn't matter.

What mattered was the here and now.

"No. They moved to Florida right after Dad retired a few years back."

He glanced across the diner at the Hernandez family, laughing and talking, and yearned to join their relaxed group. Juan and his family had moved to Bayside about a month after Nick and Connor. Juan had transferred to the auto plant nearby from a factory near Guaymas, Mexico. After a bit of a rocky start with learning the language and resettling in a new country, they'd become a beloved part of the community, with little Analia basically having the run of Bayside. Good thing too, since the auto plant had been closed now and Juan was out of work and couldn't afford to move his family back to Mexico. The community had rallied around them, making sure they had food and clothes and enough money to survive on. Juan was also working construction to make ends meet while his wife tutored high-school kids in Spanish.

"Do you know them?" Belle asked, watching the Hernandez family, as well.

"I do. Their daughter is a patient of mine," he said. "Why?"

"No reason." She shrugged and fiddled with her napkin. "Crouzon's?"

"Yep."

"How old is she?"

"Con's age."

"She should be ready for the second phase of her surgery soon," Belle said, all animosity between them gone as they discussed medicine. Funny how that worked.

"She is, but it's expensive. Analia's father lost his job and I've been working to get their case taken on pro bono by a colleague of mine in Detroit, but so far the paperwork is still tied up." Nick sighed and sipped his cherry cola. "They're doing the best they can. Analia's happy."

"Is she?" Belle glanced at the little girl again, then looked away. "Let's get back to discussing the free clinic. It's why we're here."

"The first thing we need to do is get into there and assess the state of things," he said, forcing an ease he didn't quite feel. "I'll call my PA tonight and tell her the situation. See if she can handle the patient load tomorrow by herself until we can work out a schedule."

"If repairs need to be made, we'll have to hire someone. Might be hard to get the work done on such short notice." Belle surveyed the interior of the diner as she spoke, and he tried to see it through her eyes. Far from the pristine interiors of Rodeo Drive, Pat's looked like a thrift store had exploded—local knickknacks and memorabilia covering every square inch of wall space.

"Juan Hernandez might be able to help. He does good work." He'd helped renovate the house Nick had bought after returning to Bayside. "I'll ask him if he can stop in tomorrow and take a look." Nick glanced at the calendar on the wall, donated courtesy of the local volunteer fire department. "If we get started in the morning, that gives us eight days until Christmas Eve."

"Fine. But this is all still contingent on my boss granting me an extension on my bereavement leave." She folded her hands atop the table, prim as a church lady on Sunday.

Pat set their plates down a few minutes later. "Dinner is served. Enjoy."

Nick thanked him then divided the huge burger in two and put half on Con's plate, along with half the fries, then reached for the ketchup and mustard, noticing Belle picking through her salad. "Are you going to eat your food or sort it to death?"

"I want to make sure there's no cheese or croutons hidden in here."

"You ordered it without and I'm sure Pat fixed it that way."

She kept picking and he rolled his eyes.

Belle turned her attention to Connor instead. "What do you like to do for fun?"

His son swallowed a fry, ketchup smeared on his cheek. "I play hockey."

"Really?" She gave Nick a surprised look. "So, you won't let him cross the street or order for himself, but you let him go out on the ice and risk life and limb over a puck?"

"Hockey is a very safe sport," Nick ground out, a muscle pulsating near his tense jaw. "The coach supervises the team at all times and takes every precaution to ensure the kids' safety. Besides, I played when I was his age. It's good exercise and the team-building skills he learns are essential for later in life." He gave her arch stare, as if challenging her to contradict him. For reasons he didn't want to contemplate, he wanted to get a rise out of her. Disrupt that cool exterior of hers and get her as riled up as he felt inside. "If you're so concerned for my son's well-being, Connor's got his last game for the year the day before Christmas Eve in Manistee. Come with us and check it out."

The moment the words left his mouth he wanted to take them back. Spending more time around Belle than what he'd already be doing to get the free clinic ready wasn't a good idea.

Thankfully, she turned him down anyway. "I'm sure I'll be busy preparing to reopen the clinic, but I appreciate the invitation."

Nick exhaled slowly, feeling like he'd dodged a major bullet. He chewed his burger without tasting it, glancing over to find Connor fiddling with his tablet again. Normally he banned devices at the dinner table and was about to tell his son to stow the electronics away then hesitated.

Controlling. Belle's description rubbed him wrong in all the worst place. He wasn't controlling. He was doing the best he could here, dammit.

So, instead, he bit back the reprimand for Connor and swallowed it down with another swig of cherry soda. One night of web surfing during dinner wouldn't hurt anything, right?

Belle continued nibbling her food like she was at some fancy society luncheon and not Bayside's best greasy spoon. Nick wasn't fooled by her pretension, though. She must've forgotten he'd seen her covered with mashed potatoes and dripping with cheesy macaroni after a particularly heinous food fight in the school cafeteria. Regardless of their years apart, he knew the real Belle—even if that girl now seemed buried deeper than his beloved Vicki and the future they'd planned. After Connor had been born, he'd dreamed of having more children, more family vacations, more time to just enjoy the life he and Vicki had built together. They'd not married for love, but over their time together their friendship had grown into something better—affection, support, loyalty, trust. Rare and valuable things these days. Vicki had been his go-to person for talking out his problems and sharing his victories. He'd even told her about Belle. In the big and the small ways, he and Vicki had been there for each other. Without her, he'd done his best to manage on his own, charging forward, putting one foot in front of the other each day, doing what had to be done.

Life had gone on. Different than he'd expected, but onward just the same.

"After I talk to my boss tonight, I'll come up with a list of tasks for you to handle and a schedule so we can make sure nothing gets missed," Belle said, jarring him back to the present.

Nick snorted and shook his head, focusing on his exhaustion and the grumpiness it caused, because if he didn't, he'd be too vulnerable, too raw, and that was unacceptable. "Just like old times."

"Excuse me?" Belle paused in midbite and gave him a fractious look.

"You were always bossing everyone around," he said matter-of-factly, knowing he was pushing her buttons.

"I am not bossy." She put down her fork, her movement stiff. "I simply try to show people better ways of doing things."

"Sounds bossy to me."

"Shut up."

"Make me."

And just like that they were kids again, back in Marlene's clinic, him teasing the pretty girl who'd always seemed way out of his league. Melancholy squeezed his heart again and he looked away. Dammit. He was tired, yes, but the funeral had really thrown him. He hated funerals. They always reminded him of Vicki.

They ate the rest of their meal in silence. Once they'd finished, he waited while Pat cleared their plates then tried his best to get back to normal, even though normal seemed a thousand miles away at present. "We get started in the morning, then?"

"Yes. Pending my boss's approval." She stood and slipped her coat on then belted it up. "I'll meet you in front of the clinic in the morning at nine. If something changes, I'll call you. I have your number."

Nick swiped the check before she could, flashing what he hoped was a polite smile. "My treat, Belle. We're partners now. You need a ride to your aunt's place?"

"No. I got a rental at the airport in Lansing." Belle lifted her chin and walked toward the exit, saying over her shoulder, "Thank you for dinner. Bye, Connor."

Nick lingered after she left. "You want pie, Con?"

His son grinned. "With ice cream?"

"Of course." Nick hailed Pat and ordered dessert while Analia wandered over to take the seat vacated by Belle.

"She's pretty," the little girl said, lisping due to dental issues. "What's her name?"

"Christabelle Watson. She was Marlene's niece. And she's a doctor like me."

"Wow." Analia stared at the front door while Pat delivered dessert. "Are you friends?"

"We used to be." Nick exhaled and rubbed a hand over his face, fatigue and grief threatening to overwhelm him once more. "I'm not so sure now."

"Okay. Bye." Analia said, ending the conversation

abruptly, as eight-year-olds were prone to do, and headed back to her family's table.

Nick turned back to find half the pie and ice cream already gone. As a growing kid, Connor could put away the food. Still, his son was healthy and strong and smart, and Nick said a silent prayer every night that things would stay that way. Being a doctor had good and bad sides. People joked about self-diagnosing themselves on the internet with every disease under the sun. Nick wasn't that bad, but he did like to err on the side of caution when it came to Connor. He was only being a good parent.

Belle's words looped back through his tired brain before he could stop them.

How controlling of you...

He sighed and scrubbed a hand over his face. Yeah, maybe he had been a bit overbearing, but some days it was all he had. He just wanted to protect his child, since life could be so easily lost at any time.

After they'd finished their meal and he'd paid the bill, Nick stopped on their way out to check with Juan about working on the clinic. Luckily, the guy said he was between jobs and agreed to meet him in the morning. Then Nick and Connor walked back out into the cold night air, their breath frosting as they returned to his SUV parked behind the funeral home. He spotted Belle at the funeral home across the street, scraping the windshield of the compact car she'd rented while trying not to fall on her butt in those stilettos of hers, looking just as determined as he remembered.

He turned away and pulled out his phone to call his PA about taking over for the most part until after Christmas. Hopefully, it wouldn't be a problem. Elise was always bugging him to give her a bigger role in the clinic anyway and she and her family were Jewish. Hanukkah had fallen early that year, so he felt optimistic she might help him out. The last thing he wanted to do was close during one of their busiest times of the year when the people of Bayside needed them most. The closest hospital was in Manistee, about an hour away, so anything he could treat here in town was faster and cheaper for everyone involved.

Regardless of what happened at his office, one thing was for sure.

The next two weeks would be mighty interesting.

CHAPTER TWO

BELLE PARKED IN the driveway of her aunt Marlene's modest ranch-style home on Hancock Street and stumbled inside the foyer, her feet numb and her arm aching from toting her heavy wheeled suitcase behind her. At least the ride had given her some much-needed time to herself to recalibrate. Hard to believe after all this time that he still affected her like no other man.

It made no sense whatsoever.

She'd dated plenty of men in Beverly Hills—rich, gorgeous, successful, highly desirable men. Yet not one of them had seemed to hold a candle to Nick when it came to physical attraction. Maybe because he'd been her first.

First kiss, first boyfriend, first...*everything.*

And they said you never forgot your first...

No. She shook off those unwanted thoughts and slumped back against the closed door, listening to the lonesome sound of the wind howling as the snowstorm picked up outside and the reality of her situation crept into her bones. She was back in Bayside. She was unexpectedly partnered with Nick again. She was all alone because Aunt Marlene was gone.

Forever.

The tears she'd struggled to hold back since her

arrival spilled forth as she toed off her pumps then walked into the living room, spotting all the reminders of the life she'd left behind. There was the lopsided ceramic mug she'd made for Aunt Marlene in sixth grade. And a picture of the two of them at Belle's high-school graduation. On the wall in the hallway were photos of her aunt with her patients at various local events—the July Fourth band concert in the gazebo on the town green, the annual Christmas tree lighting ceremony.

There were pictures of Belle's parents too on their wedding day. Aunt Marlene had been her mom's maid of honor. Memories of her parents were blurry and soft in Belle's mind, like watercolors. She remembered her mother making a birthday cake, her father teaching Belle how to fish for salmon in the Manistee River, their trip to Tahquamenon Falls State Park when Belle had thought the iron-rich falls were made of root beer.

Her heart ached and more tears fell. Her parents had both been doctors too. Family medicine. They'd always talked about Belle taking over their practice someday. Perhaps that was another reason she'd been so torn about choosing plastic surgery as her specialty in college. If she'd stayed with GP, it would have been another link to them, but fate had had other ideas—especially after her ill-fated trip to see Nick in college. Finding out about his engagement and his impending fatherhood had left her feeling untethered, powerless. She'd focused on the one area where she still felt like she had control—her career.

She gave a sad little ironic snort. Seemed Nick wasn't the only one with control issues.

With the back of her hand, Belle swiped at her damp cheeks. God, she missed her family. Aunt Marlene had been so young, so vital, despite her age and heart condition. She'd always seemed immortal to Belle, even though rationally she'd known someday the end would come. She'd just never expected it to happen so fast.

If only I'd known...

She hadn't, though, because Aunt Marlene had never told Belle how sick she was. That stubborn, independent streak ran in their family and had reared its ugly head again apparently. Aunt Marlene had always been the type to do for others, yet never let anyone help her in her time of need. She'd not wanted to be a bother to anyone, she'd always said.

Belle would've loved nothing more than to be bothered by her aunt just one more time.

Maybe it was being back home again after all this time, but Belle felt at a loose end and was reconsidering everything in her life. Her career, her relationships, her future. Funerals always seemed to bring out her introspective side and this one was worst of all.

When her parents had died, Belle had been a child and Aunt Marlene had made the choices for her. Now it all fell on Belle to pick up the pieces and decide how best to move forward.

Sniffling, she returned to the living room and sank down on the sofa to stare at the Christmas tree in the corner. Her aunt must have put it up before going into the hospital after Thanksgiving. Grief flooded her anew at all the memories of holidays past. The tree glowed with twinkling lights and tinsel and she finally let herself sob for all she'd lost and for the beloved aunt she'd never see again.

Pain and doubt scraped her raw inside. Sticking to her career plans had been a way of remaining close to her parents and Aunt Marlene over the years, even if she'd left Bayside and chosen a different field of practice. Her rational brain said they'd all want her to be happy, but the scared child still lurking inside her feared maybe she'd not done enough to fulfill their dreams for her. Maybe she'd not done enough to fulfill her dreams for herself.

A buzzing sound finally pulled her out of her tears and self-recriminations and back to reality. Dabbing her eyes with a tissue, Belle rushed to grab her bag from the foyer and pull out her cell phone to see an incoming video call from Dr. Reyes.

Doing her best to restore some semblance of order to her appearance, Belle tapped the screen. Dr. Reyes's tanned, perfectly sculpted face appeared. His dark eyes narrowed as she forced a smile.

"Hello, sir," Belle said, her voice still rough from crying.

"Dr. Watson, are you all right? You didn't return any of my calls today."

Belle took a deep breath, forcing her emotions down deep and switching to professional mode. "I'm fine. Thank you. Just tired."

"My condolences again on the passing of your aunt. Were you close?"

"Yes." She blinked hard against the unwanted sting of more tears. "She raised me after my parents died."

"I'm sorry. There's nothing more important than family."

At least she had the presence of mind not to point out the oddness of Dr. Reyes's statement, since he'd been married three times.

"What's the name of the town where you're staying?" he asked. "Seaport?"

"Bayside."

"Ah. I come from in a small town myself in Brazil. Five hundred people."

Belle steeled herself to declare the bad news. "There may be an issue with my return date, sir."

"What?" Dr. Reyes frowned. "Why? The standard three days to mourn and take care of your aunt's affairs should be more than sufficient, Dr. Watson. And what of the patient I'm seeing in your absence? The breast reconstruction?"

Belle winced. In all the stress of today she'd forgotten about poor Cassie Gordon. At just twenty, her young patient had already been through five previous procedures to correct what should've been a simple case of asymmetry. But now her case had become a nightmare of complications due the earlier botched surgeries by other physicians. The procedure had taken Belle three hours for what should have been forty-minute surgery. There'd been vast amounts of scar tissue to remove and internal suturing required to close things up properly. "Is Miss Gordon doing well?"

"For now." Annoyance crept into Dr. Reyes's tone. "Explain to me why you must stay."

Belle cleared her suddenly constricted throat. "There's more to do than I expected to settle my aunt's estate and I'm the only family she had left. Plus, there was a stipulation."

"A stipulation?"

"Yes. Her final wish was for us to reopen the free clinic on Christmas Eve before we liquidate the proceeds."

"We?"

Images of Nick tonight at the diner flooded Belle's mind once more before she shoved them aside. "I inherited half of my aunt's estate, along with another person."

Dr. Reyes frowned. "Splitting assets is a complicated business, but you went home to pay respects, not revive your aunt's medical practice."

"I know, sir." Bristling under the censure in his tone, Belle raised her chin. "None of this was my intention, but things are a bit more complicated than I anticipated." Her heart pinched as she remembered her aunt soldiering on through what must have been one of the most difficult times in her life on Belle's behalf all those years ago. If her aunt could do it, then she could too. "The free clinic will reopen on Christmas Eve, then I'll fly home on the holiday. I realize this is an inconvenience, but I'll work double shifts, triple even, once I return. Whatever you need."

"What I need, Dr. Watson, is to know your priorities are straight," Dr. Reyes said, then sighed. "Fine. But I expect you to be back in California on Christmas, nine days from now. Not too much to ask, I think, after everything I've done for you in your career."

His words pulled Belle up short. Yes, he'd hired Belle fresh out of residency, advising her on the ins and outs of conquering the Everest-sized mountain of Beverly Hills plastic surgery. But she'd had other lucrative offers, as well. And she'd worked hard, made a lot of sacrifices herself to get where she was. If all she'd accomplished on her own volition didn't win her the right to take sole ownership of her success, then she didn't know what did. It also made her doubts about the partnership and what she truly wanted stir more strongly inside her. Still, she was resolved to do her duty, for now. "Thank you. I appreciate your kindness."

In truth, wrapping everything up here by Christmas was pushing it, but she'd figure it out. She worked miracles on a daily basis with her patients. She'd survived losing her parents and losing the boy she'd loved back in high school. She'd survive losing Aunt Marlene too.

"Good," Dr. Reyes said, bringing her back to the present. "I'll check in with you again tomorrow re your patient."

He ended the call and she sat there staring at the Christmas tree for a long time afterward, her mind racing. For the past eighteen years she'd worked so hard to get where she was, never once stopping to look at all the things she'd missed, all the things that had slipped away or fallen by the wayside in her pursuit of success. But she loved her life, loved her work, loved the new opportunities on her horizon.

Don't I?

To be honest, it had begun to ring a bit hollow lately.

A bit lonely too.

Letting her head fall back against the cushions, Belle picked up a crocheted pillow and stared at the quote embroidered there: *Bloom where you're planted.*

Belle was trying hard to keep on blooming, even if the soil right now felt pretty rocky.

"Time for bed, Con," Nick called as he turned down the flannel sheets in his son's room. They'd picked them out a few weeks previously during a trip to the big-box store in Manistee. Goofy lime-green monsters and bright orange superheroes covered the material. Nick had been obsessed with the latest space movie characters when he'd been a kid too.

Like father, like son.

"Dad, who was the woman at dinner tonight?" Con asked as he walked into the room and climbed into bed in his pajamas, wiping toothpaste from his mouth with his sleeve. "She seemed kind of…stressed out."

"She probably was," Nick sighed as he tucked his son in. Honestly, Belle had seemed ready to shatter at any minute. The idea bothered Nick more than he cared to admit. He had no business worrying about Belle. He'd made a vow to his dying wife on the day she'd passed away—to put their son first, to keep him happy and safe. His needs came second, if at all. After everything Vicki had sacrificed to marry him, it was the least he could do. He sat on the edge of the bed. "Belle's been through a lot. Dr. Marlene was her aunt."

"Are you guys friends?" Con leaned back against the pillows resting against his headboard, looking as energetic as ever. Nick's hopes for a quick good night faded.

"We used to be. Go to sleep. You've got school in the morning." He stood and walked to the door. The past was over and bringing it up now would only lead to more questions from Connor. Questions Nick did not want to answer tonight. Maybe not ever.

Unfortunately, his son wasn't going to let the subject of Belle drop so easily. "So, why aren't you friends anymore?"

Because Belle and I have too much history. Instead, he said, "It's complicated."

His son's determination gave way to obstinacy. "Mom said talking about things made them better."

"Your mom…" Nick started, then stopped. It was true. Vicki had been a good talker. A good listener too. It was one of the reasons she and Nick had first become pals in medical school. In fact, the night Vicki had gotten pregnant, she'd been consoling Nick about his loneliness over Belle. She'd been nursing her wounds over a bad breakup herself. They'd both had too much to drink and one thing had led to another. It had been a fluke, a one-night stand, but eight weeks later Vicki had told him she was pregnant. Nick had done the noble thing, of course, and proposed. Vicki had agreed, despite the fact she'd had dreams too, had been on track for a career as a nurse practitioner in Manhattan. She'd given it all up to marry him and raise their son together.

Connor was still staring at him, waiting for his answer, so Nick did the best he could. "Your mom did like to talk things out. But she also knew when to let things rest."

"Please, Dad? I miss her. You never mention Mom anymore. I dreamed about her again last night. She was walking away and no matter how loud I screamed for her to come back, she just left me behind."

At the catch in his son's voice, Nick caved like a crumbling mine shaft. He'd thought that by not bringing Vicki up so much he'd save Connor the pain of her loss, but it seemed he'd only made things worse. Feeling like the world's worst parent ever, he toed off his shoes then climbed back onto the bed beside his son, resting against the headboard next to Connor. "Fine. You want to know about me and Belle? I'll tell you. But I'm making this quick because we both have to be up early. Got it?"

Con grinned and settled back against his favorite monster pillow. "Got it."

Nick took a deep breath. "Belle and I both volunteered after school in Marlene's clinic."

"You used to clean up blood and guts and yucky stuff? Cool!"

"No. We used to sterilize instruments and scrub down exam tables." He put an arm around Connor and tugged the boy into his side, ruffling his hair. "No gore. Well, unless you consider taking care of the parakeet cages in the lobby yucky."

"Super-yucky." His son wrinkled his nose. "Go on."

"We spent a lot of time together at the clinic, since we both wanted to be doctors. Later, Belle and I dated in high school. We were even prom king and queen."

"Wow. I'm never going to date anyone. Especially a girl."

"Never say never." Nick laughed. "Trust me."

"So, why don't you like her anymore?" Connor asked.

An uncomfortable twinge of regret pinched his chest before he tamped it down. "Nothing happened. Belle moved away from Bayside, and I did too. Our paths diverged."

"Diverged?" Con looked up at him, frowning. "What's that mean?"

"It means we ended up in different places." He rested his head back against the headboard and closed his eyes. Truth was, he'd loved Belle enough to let her go. The fact she'd shared with him all her hopes and dreams and her parents' aspirations for her had sealed the deal. He couldn't hold her back. Wouldn't hold her back.

Then he'd gone down a different path with Vicki and their destinies hadn't crossed again, until now. Belle was his past. Connor was his future. The sooner Nick got that straight, the better off he'd be. "Belle and I parted ways a long time ago, son. We're different people now."

His son seemed to consider that a moment. "And then you met Mom."

"And then I met your mother."

Connor yawned and Nick took his cue to leave. He slipped out of the bed and walked to the door again, picking up his shoes along the way. "Good night, son."

"'Night." Con snuggled down under the covers. "Hey, Dad?"

"Yeah?"

"If Belle decides to stay, would she be able to help Analia?"

Nick exhaled slowly and hung his head. "She won't stay, son. She needs to get back to California. Her life is there."

"Miracles happen all the time." Connor peered at Nick, the covers tucked beneath his chin as icy snow tapped against the window panes. "Mom used to say that too."

The chances of Belle choosing Bayside over Beverly Hills were slim to none, but it was late and Nick was tired. "We'll see. Now, get some sleep. We've got a busy day tomorrow."

"Hey, Dad?" Connor's yawn obscured the words.

Nick stopped halfway out of the room. "Yes, son?"

"When are you going to let me walk to school like Eric does?"

He sighed. The question struck far close to home after Belle's judgmental remarks earlier. He didn't want to smother Connor, but he'd do anything to keep him safe. "We'll talk about it tomorrow, okay? Now go to sleep."

"Okay," Connor said, his tone resigned. "Love you."

"Love you too, son." Nick closed the door, feeling like he'd gone ten rounds with an MMA fighter instead of put his kid to bed. When Vicki had been alive, they'd used to talk about stuff they wanted to do with Connor. Take him across the country and visit all the national parks. Let him have free rein in what he wanted to learn and do and be, within reason. Raise him to be an independent, free-thinking, fearless boy.

Now Nick watched his kid like a hawk. He didn't let Connor cross the street alone because another child had been hit last year on Main Street on his way home from school. Granted, it had been the beginning of summer and with the tourists beginning to flock to the area the number of distracted drivers on the road had increased, but it didn't reassure Nick at all. He trusted Connor. It was everyone else who made him wary. In the rational part of his mind, he knew he couldn't keep Con under his wing forever, but he wasn't sure how he'd cope if anything happened to his son.

Bone-weary, he checked the locks then shut off the lights before heading to bed himself, Belle's words still echoing through his head. He didn't want to be controlling. Back in the day, he'd gone with the flow and dealt with the punches as they came.

But as he brushed his teeth then finally climbed between the sheets, he realized life had changed him. Much as he hated to admit it, maybe he should allow Connor a little more freedom. After all, that was why he'd moved back to Bayside. The safety, the security.

Except with Belle back in town, the well-ordered life he'd tried to rebuild and protect suddenly felt threatened. He turned onto his back and stared up at the ceiling. He closed his eyes, but all he could see was Belle sitting in the diner, shiny as a new penny under the harsh fluorescent lights, and his chest squeezed with an odd mix of apprehension and anticipation.

Grumbling, he turned over and punched his pillow before burying his face in it. Hell, he wasn't sure why he was getting all riled up over her return anyway. Wasn't like he was interested in getting involved with her again. Just the opposite. For all he knew, she was seeing someone out in California. The thought nipped at him despite his wish to the contrary.

No. In a few hours he'd face her again, clear-headed

and logical this time because if he was honest, having Belle back in Bayside was far more dangerous to him than any hit-and-run driver would ever be.

CHAPTER THREE

BELLE ARRIVED AT the clinic at nine sharp the next morning, only to find Nick already there. She went inside and took off her coat, hanging it on a peg behind the receptionist's desk. The short drive from her aunt's house had done little to improve her outlook, though wearing her sturdy boots this morning had helped on the slick pavement outside. She'd slept poorly the night before, a mixture of replaying in her head the phone call with Dr. Reyes and the dinner with Nick. It had all created a swirl of insomnia she'd been unable to conquer.

Nick leaned out of one of the exam rooms down the short hallway in front of her and flashed a polite smile. "Good morning."

"What's good about it?" she mumbled. "Is there coffee?"

He strolled out, looking far better than any man had a right to in faded jeans and T-shirt hugging his muscular torso in all the right places. Belle wasn't sure why she'd expected him to show up in his lab coat again, but that would have been far preferable, and safer, than what he was wearing now. Her pulse sped as he slouched a shoulder against the wall, his ankles crossed. "I thought you liked tea."

"I do," she snapped, feeling even more out of sorts

thanks to the man across from her. "But since there isn't a decent cup in this town, I'll settle for coffee."

He disappeared back into the exam room again, emerging moments later with a cardboard tray bearing two covered cups from a shop she'd never heard of and the stout man from the diner the night before following close at his heels. Nick held out the tray to her. "I ran up to Manistee after I dropped Connor off at school this morning. Consider it my peace offering. And let me introduce you to Mr. Juan Hernandez. He's agreed to help us fix up the clinic."

Belle shook the man's hand. "Hello. You were at Pat's last night with your family."

"Yes. My wife and daughter." Juan smiled. "Analia is my little princess."

"Juan's a great carpenter. Did all the renovations on my house here in Bayside. He'll be a big help getting the clinic reopened." Nick glanced over at Belle. "If you're staying."

"I'm staying." She took one of the cups, lifting the lid to sniff the steaming liquid inside.

"It's green tea," Nick said. "You tried to order it last night, right?"

"Right." She took a sip and couldn't suppress a tiny sigh of pleasure.

"Good, huh?" The amusement twinkling in his warm brown eyes had her turning away fast. His continued effect on her was crazy. Stupid. Beyond inconvenient, considering they had exactly eight days until they reopened the clinic on Christmas Eve. After that, she'd be on the first plane back to California. She took another swallow of tea for fortitude. "This is very good. Thank you. Dr. Reyes gave me an extension on my bereavement leave through Christmas Eve. We have a little over a week to get the clinic ready to reopen. Thus, we need a plan."

"'Thus, we need a plan,'" Nick parroted back to her. "Since when do you say 'thus'?"

"People change." She walked around the receptionist desk, trailing her finger though a thick coating of dust. The paint on the walls was faded and the carpets were worn. The ceiling tiles above sported a few water stains, as well. One of the fluorescent lights popped and hissed ominously and a strange wheezing noise echoed from the heating vent above the desk. All in all, the place was a mess. "You weren't kidding about the clinic being run-down."

"When Marlene's health took a turn for the worse, she had a hard time keeping up. I offered to help her, but she refused," Nick said. "You know how she was. Always doing for other people, never accepting assistance herself."

"Yes." Belle headed down to check out the three exam rooms. The equipment had to be as old as she was. It was going to take a massive effort to get this all up to snuff. Good thing her can-do attitude was what had gotten her where she was today.

"Juan will oversee the repairs and any issues with the heating and electrical. What he can't fix himself, he knows the people who can. My PA's agreed to take on extra patients, which allows me to split my time between this place and my office." Nick stepped into the small exam room behind her, his warmth surrounding her. "And my office manager, Jeanette, volunteered to handle the front-desk duties at the free clinic, so we can check that off the list. Between all of us, we should have all the boxes checked."

Juan excused himself to inspect the rest of the clinic

and Belle blinked at the anatomy poster on the wall, the paper yellowing around the edges. It had hung there for as long as she could remember.

"I just have one remaining question," Nick said.

Belle looked back at him over her shoulder. "What?"

"Yesterday, you were all about leaving. What changed your mind?"

When she hadn't been able to sleep the night before, she'd gone through more of her aunt's things. Photos, letters, mementos. All of it had reminded Belle how much Aunt Marlene had loved this place. How much she'd loved Belle too. It had been enough to make Belle determined to see her aunt's last wishes fulfilled, no matter how difficult it might be to have Nick hovering around her for the next two weeks. "You were right. My aunt deserves better. If reopening the free clinic one last time was important to her, I'll make it happen."

"Hmm." Nick stepped closer and her pulse kicked up a notch. "Say that again."

Belle frowned. "If reopening the clinic is important—"

"No. The other part."

"What other part?"

"Where you said I was right. I don't hear it often enough. Especially from you."

"Too bad." Belle walked out of the exam room and headed for the lobby once more, doing her best to focus on the job ahead and not the irritating man behind her. "We need to make a list of supplies to order, both cleaning and medical."

"I can take care of the medical part." Nick shrugged. "I have a shipment coming in for my practice next Monday. We can take what we need from that then I'll restock again after Christmas. It's only for one day, so we should have plenty to cover both clinics."

"Okay. Then I'll stop by the store in Manistee and pick up cleaning supplies when I go to the hospital later to spread the word about the clinic. Maybe I'll stop by the office supply place too and have some flyers made up so we can post them around town to help us spread the word."

"Sounds good." Nick grinned. "Maybe we could see about doing a little promo at the Chamber of Commerce Holiday Ball next week, as well. I can talk to the mayor's office."

"Great. I need to be there anyway to accept Aunt Marlene's award."

"Right. We could go together, schmooze the locals, build some buzz for the clinic."

It almost felt like old times, back when they'd both worked here after school, but she stopped herself. This was all only temporary. Things were different now. The sooner she remembered that, the better. She looked at Nick again for a moment before grabbing her coat. "Maybe. I should probably get going up to Manistee."

"But you just got here," he started, only to be interrupted by the front door opening.

A beautiful woman about Belle's age, with long dark hair and sparkling onyx eyes walked in holding the hand of the little girl with Crouzon syndrome from the night before.

"I know you," the little girl said, her words slightly lisped. She pulled free from her mother and headed for Belle. "You were at Pat's last night. You're pretty."

"Thank you." Belle crouched in front of the child. "What's your name?"

"Analia," the little girl said, reaching out to touch Belle's red coat. "Red's my favorite color."

"Mine too." Up close, she studied the little girl's features—wide-set and bulging eyes, beaked nose, and an underdeveloped upper jaw. Classic Crouzon's. The premature fusion of certain skull bones had resulted in the abnormal shape of the girl's head and face. Nick had mentioned breathing problems too. Not uncommon. Belle had worked with two children with similar cases back in California, performing the complicated surgery and follow-ups to correct problems like Analia's. Too bad she wouldn't be here long enough this time.

Her heart tugged as she straightened. Part of her wanted to throw caution to the wind and take the case anyway. It would be simple enough to do a consult and examination, obtain the necessary releases, then book an OR in Manistee. But she already had more than enough on her plate to keep her busy during her short stay in Bayside and Nick had mentioned working the little girl in with his colleague in Detroit. The most prudent course of action was to let him handle it.

Instead, she introduced herself to Analia's mother. "Dr. Watson. Please call me Belle."

"Rosa Hernandez." The woman's grip was firm and sure. "We came to take my husband to breakfast, if you can spare him for an hour or so."

"I think we can," Nick said, calling over his shoulder. "Juan, your family's here."

The guy came out and picked up Analia, hugging her tight before kissing his wife. "I'll be back. After we eat, I'll swing by the hardware store and pick up what I need to get started."

Belle watched them leave, then turned back to Nick. "She needs the surgery done."

"She does. Too bad you won't be sticking around." Nick flinched. "Sorry. I shouldn't have said anything. I know you've got other commitments."

Hurt pinched her chest. He made the word *commitments* sound more like *excuses*. "The procedure required to correct her abnormalities is major. Wires on her jaw for at least a month to spur new bone growth. She'd have to wear a halo device for at least four months to stabilize everything. It wouldn't be fair of me to take a case, Nick, knowing I wouldn't be around to see it through. My time in Bayside is limited. I need to be honest about what I can and can't do here."

"You're right." He sighed and turned away, wandering back down the hall. "Drive safely to Manistee. I'll see you when you get back."

Belle grabbed her bag then left the clinic, feeling like she was caught in a trap with no safe way out.

Nick spent the rest of his day dealing with what felt like one emergency after another. Turned out all those water stains on the ceiling tiles were due to a pipe with a slow leak in the ceiling. Juan had no more than gotten a plumber there to correct the problem than his PA called.

"Sorry to bother you, but I'm afraid I've got a suspected case of bacterial meningitis."

"Damn." Nick's heart sped. Meningitis was highly contagious and would require reporting to the local Board of Health. He prayed it wasn't someone from Connor's school. "Who's the patient?"

"Lisa Merkel, age twelve. Homeschooled," the PA said. The knot of tension between Nick's shoulder blades eased slightly. "Patient has a high fever, stiff neck, headache, and nausea."

He scrubbed a hand over his face. "I'm on my way."

After letting Juan know he was leaving, Nick raced over to his offices. The white limestone exterior of the building gleamed in the sunshine as he pulled into his reserved spot. He walked in, still dressed in jeans and a sweatshirt but slipped on a lab coat to look more professional before going in to see the Merkels.

The parents were understandably upset, and poor Lisa looked horrible, her face pale and clammy and her body racked with shivers from the fever. Nick went over the chart and immediately called an ambulance to transport the girl to the hospital in Manistee. After talking with the ER doc on duty about the case, he went back into the exam room to console the parents until the EMTs arrived.

"We'll do everything we can to help her. The ER at Manistee General is prepared for her arrival. The doc there will do a lumbar puncture to confirm the meningitis then begin antibiotics prophylactically while we wait for the results. She's in good hands."

By the time he made it home that night it was well past ten and Connor was already asleep. He sent the sitter home then slumped down on the sofa in his living room, the TV droning in the background. Medicine wasn't a nine-to-five job and he was grateful to have found Mollie to watch his son. She was an older woman whose husband had passed away a few years before Nick had moved back to Bayside. She loved Connor almost as much as Nick did and treated the little boy like one of her grandsons.

After a yawn and a stretch, Nick got up and wandered upstairs to Con's room, sneaking over to give the kid a kiss, narrowly avoiding tripping over the toys and hockey equipment strewn across the floor, before he headed back down to the kitchen to fix himself some dinner.

Bless Mollie's heart, she'd left him a plate of homemade chicken and dumplings in the fridge. The dish was Connor's favorite. Nick popped it into the microwave then got a glass of water to drink. As he waited for his food to heat, he felt a weird pang in his chest.

Not sadness. Not grief over Marlene either.

Loneliness. That's what it was. Except he didn't have any business feeling lonely.

He'd chosen his path and he was at peace with it.

Aren't I?

The microwave beeped and he took out his food, then grabbed a fork and a napkin before carrying it all back into the living room to eat in front of the TV. He should be used to it by now. Vicki had been gone nearly two years. He'd made the right choice.

Then an image of Belle from earlier popped into his head.

He'd been glad to see she'd dressed more sensibly in jeans and a sweater and boots. A vast improvement from the day before. In fact, she'd almost reminded him of the old Belle—same killer curves, same killer smile, same sweet, clean scent...

No. No, no, no.

Nick squeezed his eyes shut as new images flashed into his brain. Vicki's last days in the oncology unit, her once strong, healthy body ravaged by ovarian cancer, her once bright eyes dimmed by pain and medication. She'd given up so much for him. He couldn't forget his vow.

Not now.

He shoveled more food into his mouth and scowled at the TV.

Never mind Belle all but had a flashing neon sign above her head warning him to stay away. He was done with relationships. He was happy alone. He had his work, his patients, his son. And if sometimes it felt like something—someone—was missing, then that was his penance.

It was all good.

Is it, though?

Yes. Yes, it was. Because it had to be.

He devoured more food, staring at the news without really listening. His cell phone buzzed on the coffee table and the number for the lab at the Manistee hospital flashed on the caller ID. Nick hit redial then listened as the tech rattled off the results of Lisa's bloodwork and lumbar puncture. Positive for bacterial meningitis. Manistee General would handle filing the necessary reports with the local Board of Health. He finished up with the tech then called Lisa's parents.

"The ER doctor told us they've got Lisa on the highest does of antibiotics possible for her age." Mrs. Merkel sniffled into the phone. "We homeschooled her because we thought she'd be safer. We just wanted to keep her secure and happy."

Nick's heart went out to them, the situation hitting far too close to home. "Don't blame yourself. Lisa's in the best possible hands. They'll keep her well hydrated to bring down her fever and watch her closely. Lisa's young and strong and otherwise healthy. There's no reason she shouldn't pull through this. Try and get some rest. She'll need your support as she recovers."

He went over what to expect for the next few days and answered all of their questions then ended the call.

Nick sat there a moment afterward. By then, the rest of his dinner was cold. Just as well, since he'd lost his appetite anyway. He took his dishes to the kitchen and cleaned up before going to bed and attempting to read a new medical journal he'd had sitting around for weeks, but his concentration was shot.

After half an hour he turned off the lights. Sleep eluded him, despite his fatigue. He closed his eyes, running through Lisa's case and the work to be done at the clinic. Belle kept resurfacing in his head too, regardless of his wishes to the contrary.

Guilt gurgled inside him before he tamped it down fast.

This wasn't about attraction. Belle was a challenge. That was all. The same as working on the clinic during the holiday season, which was still hard for Nick. The strange wave of excitement he felt around Belle was nothing more than relief at being knocked out of the rut his life had fallen into lately.

Isn't it?

CHAPTER FOUR

THE NEXT MORNING Belle walked into the clinic at seven thirty sharp, happy to see she was the first one there this time. She set the travel cups of hot tea on the counter and put the bags slung over her arms on the floor. She'd brewed the tea herself at Aunt Marlene's house on the new tea-maker she'd bought in Manistee. She'd also picked up some Christmas decorations for the clinic.

Belle flipped on the lights then stared at a large hole cut into the ceiling tiles and the "Wet Floor" hazard signs placed around a ladder extending into said hole. Yikes. Nick hadn't mentioned anything wrong when she'd texted him yesterday, but something was obviously awry.

She'd just taken off her coat when a portly man in a navy blue hoodie and knit skullcap walked in.

"I'm sorry, sir, but we're not open for business yet," Belle said, startled.

"I ain't sick, lady. I'm here to fix your pipes." The guy hiked up his pants as he walked past her, then climbed the ladder to the ceiling, his top half disappearing into the hole.

Before she could ask him to explain exactly what the problem was, the front door opened again and Nick entered, looking as gorgeous as ever in clean jeans and

T-shirt, despite the dark circles beneath his eyes. Juan Hernandez came in too, giving Belle a quick wave of greeting before talking with the plumber.

"Good morning." Belle shoved a travel mug into Nick's hand. "You look like hell."

"Thanks," he said, his tone dry. "You always did know how to make a guy feel better. Must be why you're a doctor, huh?"

She ignored his sarcasm and unpacked the decorations instead. There were garlands and ornaments and red bows and sprigs of holly. She stacked them all neatly on the counter before reaching for the last bag and pulling out a box containing a small prelit Christmas tree. Minutes later she had it set up in the corner of the lobby. Belle plugged it in and fluffed the artificial branches before standing back to observe her work. Not exactly the North Pole, but the place looked a bit more festive already. She glanced at Nick, who was looking more Grinch-like by the second as he stared at the tree.

"What?" she asked.

"Nothing. I just prefer real ones."

"Well, when you buy the decorations, you can get what you like." She walked around him to pull a clipboard and pen out of her tote bag. "I'm going to take inventory. What are you doing?"

"Well, besides checking in on my patient with meningitis and helping Juan where I can, I'll be cleaning the carpets and prepping the walls for a fresh coat of paint."

"Right." Belle tucked her hair behind her ear. A patient with meningitis took a lot of time and attention. No wonder he looked tired today. Unwanted sympathy swelled inside her. Feeling sorry for Nick could lead to other feelings and that was a road best not traveled. "I'm sorry about your patient with meningitis."

"Thank you. She's doing better this morning. The antibiotics seem to be working, and her fever's down. Hopefully, she's out of the woods. And thanks for the tea." He took a sip. "This is good. Not green, though."

"Peppermint. Bought the leaves in town yesterday."

"How very Santa of you." Nick took off his coat and hung it up beside hers. "Sorry. Didn't mean to be a grouch earlier. You know how it is with an involved case."

"I do." Belle smiled, glad to have found some common ground again. "I've been getting updates on one of my patients back in California. A twenty-year-old woman I'd performed a breast augmentation on right before coming here. The case was complicated, to say the least."

"Because of her age?" Nick leaned a hip against the reception desk and watched her over the rim of his cup. "Twenty's awfully young for plastic surgery, isn't it?"

"Yes, but this patient was born with severe breast asymmetry. Unfortunately, the condition only worsened following several botched procedures by previous, underqualified surgeons." Anger fizzed in her bloodstream before she tamped it down. "Nothing makes me more furious than physicians taking a case simply because of greed. It's unforgivable."

"Wow." Nick's eyes widened. "I hope she sued."

"She might. And I'd back her up all the way." Belle exhaled, forcing her tense shoulders to relax. "Sorry. It's a pet peeve of mine."

"You were always a champion for the underdog." Nick winked at her. "Glad to see that hasn't changed."

"Thanks." At his unexpected compliment, heat prickled her cheeks. Dr. Reyes took her talents for granted. Then again, she didn't need constant praise. Doing good work was its own reward. But it was still nice to be appreciated. She took a long swig of her own tea, the peppermint sparkling on her tongue and clearing her sinuses. "Normally a breast augmentation takes me forty minutes. This poor patient's surgery took three hours because of all the scar tissue. One hundred and fifty stiches to close up the internal damage. She's doing well now, though, thank goodness. Dr. Reyes says she's very happy with the results."

"This Dr. Reyes is the head of your practice?" Nick's dark hair was still damp from a recent shower and there was a tiny red spot on his jaw where he'd cut himself shaving. The comfortable, relaxed picture he presented was far too endearing for Belle's comfort.

"Yes. Hired me straight out of residency." Already off-kilter because of her unwanted attraction to the man before her, the mention of residency only discombobulated Belle further. Memories of her ill-fated trip to see Nick caused the words to catch in her throat. From his lack of reaction, he had no idea she'd gone to visit him. It was probably for the best. It didn't matter now anyway. They were partners in this clinic venture. Nothing more. Never mind her racing pulse and wobbling knees whenever he was close. Belle headed down the hall, away from temptation. "Time to get to work."

Ugh. Whatever hormones were causing her emotional awareness of him had better clear up fast. She bustled from exam room to exam room, checking drawers and opening cabinets, making notes on her clipboard, falling into an old routine. Organization had always been one of her strong suits. She remembered keeping things in line for Aunt Marlene when she'd worked here as a teenager.

From out in the hallway the sounds of the plumber working mixed with the lilt of Juan's Spanish as he spoke to someone on the phone, presumably his wife based on the endearments he was using. Being bilingual in California was almost a given in her profession and though she did her best not to eavesdrop, Belle couldn't help picking up Analia's name and the words *too expensive*.

Her chest tightened. Given the little girl's age and breathing impairments, it would be the optimal time to do the operation. Perhaps a diagnosis of OSP—obstructive sleep apnea—would help speed the insurance company's approval. The condition was common enough in children with Crouzon's and could be life-threatening if left untreated.

"Excuse me," Nick said, scooting past her in the exam room, measuring tape in hand. "Trying to calculate out how much paint we'll need to cover the walls."

"Sure." She met his gaze before he looked away.

"So, are you dating anyone?" he asked a moment later out of the blue.

"No," she said, a bit taken aback. "I have my reasons for being single. And you?"

"Ditto."

Conversation lagged and Belle had no intention of delving deeper into their personal lives. She had enough trouble keeping her thoughts from straying to Nick whenever he was around. She changed subjects instead. "Does Analia suffer from sleep apnea?"

"Yes. She uses a CPAP machine at night because of it." Nick made a few measurements and jotted the numbers down before facing her once more. "Why?"

"If you diagnosed her with OSP, it might be enough to get her surgery approved by the insurance company." Belle leaned back against the counter, her analytical mind working overtime. "Unless you've already tried that."

"I haven't, because Juan's insurance disappeared along with his job. The Medicaid paperwork is a nightmare and with the holidays everything's on hold." He sighed. "She hasn't even been evaluated by a plastic surgeon yet. I'd like to speed things along, but it is what it is."

In her mind, Belle could already picture doing the LeFort III operation to fix little Analia's deformities—and that wasn't good. Dr. Reyes's words echoed in her head again.

You went home to pay respects to your aunt, not revive her medical practice...

Belle needed to remind herself of her duties, no matter how much she wanted to help one small girl.

"Analia's one of the bravest people I know," Nick said, a spark of admiration flaring in his gaze. Belle had forgotten how expressive his eyes were. He could say more with a look than most people could say in three days. "There are days I wish I had a quarter of her chutzpah."

Belle chuckled. She didn't know Analia well, but even she'd seen the girl's confidence and joy. "Agreed."

A moment passed between them as they watched each other over the span of a few feet. Nick's gaze flicked from Belle's eyes to her lips and she felt his look like a physical caress. Then there was a loud thud in the hallway, followed by an equally loud curse from the plumber, and the spell was broken.

Nick tensed and turned away. "Don't worry about Analia. We'll get by fine on our own."

Belle got the feeling he was talking about more than his patient. In fact, one of the first things she'd picked up on with new Nick was his isolation. Sure, he was polite enough around her, for the most part, but she sensed he kept a part of himself locked away these days. She wondered if it was because of his wife's death but didn't feel comfortable enough to ask.

Nick continued to take his measurements and she couldn't help glancing his way before forcing her attention back to her clipboard. Being so close to him again was messing with her head. She should get things done here and move on before he noticed her staring.

"Maybe you'd like to stop by Aunt Marlene's place and see if there's anything you'd like to keep. I'm trying to clear the house out for the realtor, and whatever's left over I'll have to sell. It would make things easier if there was less to deal with. I could make dinner."

Nick stopped and gave her a long look.

"What? It's dinner. We get together, eat."

"I know how dinner works, Belle," he said, reaching past her to grab a paper towel from the dispenser. His arm brushed hers and a sudden urge to put her arms around him and hold him close and bury her face in his chest like she used to threatened to take Belle under. If she rose on tiptoe, she could kiss his mouth, his neck, nuzzle the spot below his ear that used to drive him wild…

Oh, God.

"Let me ask you something," Nick said. "Why are you being so nice to me today?"

"Because we'll be working together and we might as well make the best of it," she said, her mind racing to come up with a plausible non-X-rated excuse. "And because it's the holidays and because it's rather lonely sitting in my aunt's house alone."

She hadn't meant to confess the last part, but there it was. Her face flushed hotter.

A shadow crossed his handsome face before he sighed. "I'm not sure it's good idea."

Belle bristled under his rejection. "Whatever. I was only trying to be friendly. Forget it. Should've known better."

"What's that supposed to mean?" His posture stiffened.

"Exactly what I said. Nice doesn't work with you, does it? I've been nice to you all my life and where did it get me? Nowhere."

"Hey. Wait a minute." Nick raked a hand through his dark hair and shook his head. "Look, I'm sorry things didn't work out between us back in high school, but going our separate ways was best for both of us."

Belle snorted. "Well, it certainly worked out for you, didn't it? You couldn't wait to get rid of me so you could move on."

A small muscle pulsed in his cheek and his gaze burned into her. "You want to do this now? Fine. All I ever heard from you growing up was how important a career in medicine was to you, how it made you feel connected with your parents, how it helped you stay close to them. Being with me would've destroyed the future you were meant to have. You went off to California and never looked back. Tell me it's not true, Belle."

She wanted to tell him about her impromptu visit all those years ago but couldn't bring herself to do it. The old knot of betrayal inside her tightened and once again she bit back her confession. Now wasn't the time or the place. Belle walked out instead. "I need to finish decorating the lobby."

* * *

Considering his focus was split between his work and the woman busy turning Marlene's old clinic into a Christmas wonderland, Nick got a lot more accomplished than he'd expected. He'd calculated their paint needs and paid the plumber, even lent Juan a hand and drove to the local hardware store to pick up enough new ceiling tiles to replace the stained ones. Then he'd checked in with his PA and with the hospital in Manistee on Lisa's case. Finally, he'd moved on to patching holes in the drywall, taping off the trim, and getting everything ready for the next day's painting. The manual labor helped work out the tightness in his muscles, though none of it kept his earlier conversation with Belle from replaying in his head on an endless loop.

He should've just let it go, but then she'd reacted so strangely to his question and now his interest was piqued. He hadn't been lying when he'd said she'd talked constantly about her parents and making them proud when she was a kid. Nick got it. He did. Unexpected separations made people cling to what had been lost.

An annoying whisper started in his head.

Dammit. His situation with Vicki was different. Belle's parents had died when she was a kid. She'd had no control over what had happened to them. He and Vicki had been adults. She'd given up a promising future to be with him and raise Connor together. And, while she'd never once mentioned regretting her choice, he felt guilty just the same. Maybe if she hadn't married him, hadn't had Connor and moved to Atlanta, she might still be alive.

Pressure built at the back of his skull and he slammed a lid on those ideas fast.

The physician in him knew it was baseless. Ovarian cancer was one of the most difficult to detect, often spreading to the abdomen and pelvis before it was ever detected. It was also often symptomless, so the victim didn't know they had it until it was too late. Chances were high Vicki would've succumbed to the disease whether she'd married him or not.

But at least she could have achieved her goals in her career.

Dammit. His heart clenched. This wasn't doing him any good at all. He glanced at the clock on the wall. Almost time to pick Connor up from hockey practice at school. The kid had been bouncing off the walls this morning. Today was Con's last day before holiday break and he hadn't stopped chattering about the Christmas tree lighting celebration on the town green later that night. It was a Bayside tradition.

As Nick put away the ladder, he couldn't help remembering going to the tree lighting ceremony himself as a kid. Back in the day, he and Belle had helped Marlene host the event and had even flipped the switch one year, transforming their little town into a sparkling fairy tale. Since he'd returned to Bayside, Nick hadn't really done much beyond the usual stuff at home for the holidays, other than driving by so Con could see the tree lit. This year, though, he felt an unaccountable urge to experience it all again. The community band, the huge Douglas fir decorated in lights and tinsel.

If he wanted to make it on time he'd better get a move on, especially since they needed to eat beforehand. After shutting down the rooms in the back, he headed up to the lobby. The light outside was fading already as the shortest day of the year quickly approached. It lent a sense of urgency to the already near-impossible timeline for reopening the clinic.

At the end of the hall, he caught sight of Belle teetering on one of the vinyl chairs in the lobby, doing her best to hang garland and tinsel from the ceiling. For most of the afternoon, she'd carried the clipboard around in front of her like a shield, but there was nothing preventing her from toppling off the arms of a wobbly chair and breaking her neck.

Without thinking, Nick rushed over and grabbed her hips to steady her as she rose on tiptoe to tuck a length of garland through the bars securing the new tiles to the ceiling. At his touch she froze, staring down at him with wide green eyes. "What are you—"

Sure enough, the old vinyl chair gave an ominous creak and tilted sideways, sending Belle careening against Nick and knocking him back a step. He held her tight against him and moved toward the reception desk, her floral shampoo teasing his nose.

"Put me down, please," she said, her voice muffled by his shoulder.

He did as she asked, setting her on her feet then releasing her, his pulse thudding and his mouth as dry as sandpaper. Nick shoved his hands into the back pockets of his jeans so she wouldn't see them shake as adrenaline pumped hot and fierce through his bloodstream.

She'd slipped. He'd caught her before she fell. That was all.

Why then did he feel sweaty and stunned and swirling with energy?

"Thanks." She dusted the white powder from the ceiling tiles off her hands. "Guess using the chair wasn't such a good idea."

"No, it wasn't." His words emerged harsher than he'd intended, but she could've been hurt or worse...

Vicki's face flashed into his mind. The slow beep, beep, beep of the heart monitor until it flatlined. Nick scrubbed his hands over his face, making the connection. Belle could've died.

And it would've been his fault. Again. Just like Vicki.

"Hey," she said, moving closer to him. The touch of her hand felt cool on the heated skin. "It's okay. I'm fine. You saved the day."

He shook his head and turned away. "Except I didn't."

Nick paced for a minute as he gathered the tattered shreds of his composure. God, he was a complete wreck. He walked behind the reception desk and grabbed a bottle of water from the stash beneath the counter, drinking half a bottle before focusing on Belle again. She was still standing there, watching him, her expression concerned. The last thing he wanted right now was her pity. "Tell me about Beverly Hills."

She seemed surprised. "What do you want to know?"

"What's your practice like? Is it what you expected? How's your patient load?" He set the water aside and leaned his palms on the desktop, feeling a modicum of his control returning. "I don't remember you ever expressing an interest in making people more beautiful."

She walked over to right the toppled chair. "That's not why I chose my specialty."

"Why, then?" Nick tilted his head to the side, far more interested in her answer than was wise. He wanted to know what had changed her, what had made her into the person who stood before him today.

She fiddled with one of the numerous decals of elves and ornaments and stars and gifts she'd stuck all over the front windows and he couldn't stop recalling the Christmas Eve they'd spent together eighteen years before. He'd held Belle in his arms beneath the stars at the top of the sand dunes, listening to the waves on Lake Michigan in the distance. That was the night she'd told him about her scholarship offer from UCLA and how she wasn't going to accept it because it would be too far away from home and from him. The night that had changed Nick's life forever and put him on the path he followed now.

Belle glanced back at him. "I thought we weren't discussing the past."

Damn. She had him there. Nick hung his head. "What else are we going to talk about?"

"We could just not talk at all."

"Sure. Because silence is so much less awkward."

Her gaze held his for a long moment then she smiled. It transformed her from beautiful to stunning, and for a second Nick's guilt evaporated, replaced instead by a yearning that had never entirely disappeared, even after all these years. Want danced through him like sparks from a fire. He still remembered what it felt like holding her, stroking her, nuzzling her neck, her breasts, her...

"Hello?" Belle said, breaking him out of his thoughts. "Earth to Nick."

Reality crashed back onto him like a ton of iron bricks.

He wondered how he could forget his promise so easily. He was a loner now. A father. A doctor. Belle had her own life, her own career back in California. She'd be gone after Christmas and he'd still be here in Bayside, with a thriving practice to run and a growing son to raise.

"Sorry. Thinking about my meningitis case," he lied.

She gave him a skeptical look, as if she knew it, then began neatly stacking her inventory lists on the counter and stapling the corner. "Any new updates?"

"My patient's still stable. It's a good sign, but I don't want to be too optimistic too soon." Nick crossed his arms, determined to keep things strictly platonic between him and Belle.

Because that's what he wanted.

Wasn't it?

"I'm taking off for the night," Juan said, coming out of the utility room in the back, raising a hand toward them as he exited.

"Say hello to Analia for me," Belle called, smiling.

"Will do." Juan waved. "See you both in the morning. Going to the tree lighting tonight. See you there, Nick?"

"Yep." He glanced at the clock then grabbed his coat off the rack Nick turned to face Belle again as he shrugged into his jacket. "I need to get to the school to pick up Con."

"Sure." Belle continued stapling more papers. "Have fun."

Her tone held a hint of wistful sadness and his tired heart ached. He didn't like being so conflicted, especially with everything else they were dealing with. Maybe it was time they called a truce. "Why don't you come with us?"

"Huh?" Her brows lifted in surprise. "You mean to the tree lighting ceremony?"

"Yeah." They'd go as friends. Two lonely people keeping each other company. Nothing more. He took her coat off the rack and held it for her to slip into. As she did, his fingertips grazed the soft skin at the nape of her neck. Frissons of electric awareness zinged up his arm before he could stop them. He forced an ease he didn't quite feel, turning on the charm. "I guarantee you'll have fun."

"I can't." She grabbed her bag and papers off the desk. "I really need to get these over to your office to make sure we have our supplies on time for the free clinic."

"Not a problem." He snatched the list from her and tucked the papers in his coat pocket. "I'll deliver them to Jeanette myself. C'mon. It'll make me happy."

With a shock, he realized it was true.

She tilted her head, clearly overthinking it, the same as him. "I don't want to be out late."

"We'll be back early, I promise. Con has a nine o'clock curfew anyway. He's got to be up early tomorrow for hockey." Nick held the front door for her then shut off the lights before joining Belle on the sidewalk and locking up the clinic. He hoped to keep her talking so he didn't have to think about the pounding of blood in his head and the poignant yearning in his heart. "Good. It's settled, then."

CHAPTER FIVE

BELLE CLICKED HER seat belt into place as Nick finished scraping the frost off his windshield then climbed back in behind the wheel of his SUV. The vehicle was like him—steadfast, reliable, well maintained. A no-nonsense vehicle for a no-nonsense man. So different from the ritzy sports cars and convertibles people drove around in Beverly Hills. Inside, it was warm and cozy and felt like their own private universe.

"So," he said as he started the engine and shifted into gear, "you didn't answer my question. Why plastic surgery?"

Belle shrugged and stared out the window, reliving her visit to Northwestern for the umpteenth time in her head. The sight of Nick and his bride-to-be from across the room. They'd looked so happy. She told him half the story, keeping the most painful parts to herself. "I observed a facial reconstruction on a child with a cleft palate during one of my rotations and I was hooked. The ability to create normalcy for someone who's never had it felt like a true calling. I was accepted to the fellowship program at Harvard and the rest is history." She squinted out the window at the passing scenery as they pulled onto Main Street. "Dr. Reyes was a visiting surgeon at Mass General and he approached me about joining his practice after observing my work. It was an opportunity I couldn't pass up."

Nick frowned slightly. "Isn't Beverly Hills super competitive, though?"

"Very." She smiled. "I remember telling my professors at Harvard about my decision to accept the offer and they thought I was crazy. But I chose my practice because I wanted to climb to the top of the mountain. I wanted to conquer it."

"And have you?"

"In some ways. I've built a reputation. Dr. Reyes has even offered me a partnership." Her smile faded slightly, and she looked away. "As long as I'm back in California by Christmas."

She did her best to keep the uncertainty from her tone and failed, if the look Nick gave her was any indication. "You're happy, then? It's everything you ever wanted?"

"Hmm." She tucked her hair behind her ear. "What about you? I'm sorry about your wife passing away. I don't think I ever expressed my condolences."

"Thank you." His sounded strained and Belle could've kicked herself for bringing it up. He squinted out the windshield, his face taut. "Losing Vicki was a big wake-up call."

With the door to the past wide open now, Belle couldn't help her curiosity. "Was her death the reason you gave up your practice in Atlanta moved back to Bayside?"

"Partly. I wanted Connor to grow up in the kind of place I did as a kid. Where you can go outside at night and leave your door unlocked and not worry about getting shot or robbed. Plus, I missed the community here.

And since he's my top priority now, I wanted to do what was best for him."

"And was it the best thing for you too?" He'd said he had his reasons for being single, but perhaps his went beyond the norm. One of the doctors in her practice had lost his wife a few years back and he was already re-married. She sensed there was more behind Nick's state-ment than he was letting on, but she had to tread lightly to avoid him shutting her down completely. "Must be hard, raising a child on your own. I know Aunt Marlene struggled sometimes with me, growing up."

"It can be hard." He slowed for a red light. "But I do my best."

"Connor seems like a great kid. You've done well with him."

"He's awesome."

She rested her head back against the seat and stared out at the snowy landscape. The sky above was over-cast and gray. "What about you? Why did you choose pediatrics?"

Nick accelerated once the light turned green. "After seven years of residency in Chicago." At her question-ing look, he added, "Three in GP and four in pediatric surgery, I was ready for warmer weather. The head of my practice in Atlanta was consulting on a patient in Chicago and I assisted him with a surgery. He remem-bered me. When he called to offer me a spot at the end of my residency, it was a godsend. By then Vicki was pregnant with Connor and we needed financial stabil-ity. Atlanta gave me those things."

Belle turned away so he wouldn't see her wince, but it was too late.

"What?" he asked, frowning. "What's wrong?"

She sighed and decided to come out with it. "I never

told you this, but I came to see you at Northwestern, right before I entered my fellowship at Harvard."

"What?" Nick scowled. "Why?"

"I wanted to get your opinion on what I should choose as my specialty." She shrugged, her heart threatening to beat out of her ribcage. "You were always my best sounding board. Anyway, when I got to the common area of your apartment complex, there was a celebration going on, an engagement party. I saw the happy couple was you and your soon-to-be wife. Her baby bump was evident. I left." She shook her head and stared down at her hands in her lap, blinking away tears. "I never should've come. You'd moved on. I realized I needed to do the same."

Nick looked flummoxed. "I don't know what to say, Belle. I figured you'd forgotten all about me by then."

"I should have, but I couldn't." She exhaled slowly, allowing herself to feel the pain of that long-ago night in the hope she could clear it away for good. "Part of the reason you broke up with me was because you didn't want to think about marriage or children before you were out of residency and working in private practice."

"True." The word emerged low and gruff. "But I didn't plan what happened with Vicki. We'd both had too much to drink and one thing led to another and…" He shook his head. "I'm not proud of it. But once she found out she was pregnant I couldn't abandon my responsibilities. The baby gave me a new perspective, a new future. One I'd never expected, but Vicki was a good wife and an excellent mother. She gave up everything to be with me. When she died, I promised to put Connor first, make sure he was happy and safe, so her sacrifice wasn't in vain. I came home to Bayside and set up practice. It's good, though. I make a real difference here. Money can't buy everything."

Belle mulled over his answer. "Are you happy?"

"My happiness doesn't matter. It's all about my son now."

She stared at his profile a moment, tension stinging inside her like a thousand wasps. She had so many emotions, so many more questions. With the truth out there, where did they stand? Could they have a future together after all they'd been through? Did she even want to try? Would they still fit like two pieces of the same puzzle?

The possibilities left her reeling.

They drove past a picturesque row of old Victorian-style homes decorated for the holidays. Nick made a left on Hancock Street, past her aunt's place and down two more blocks to the newly constructed Bayside Elementary, where kids swarmed across the parking lot, heading for yellow buses parked near the doors or the line of cars with parents waiting at the curb.

As their vehicle inched toward the front entrance where Connor waited with a backpack slung over one shoulder and a bag of gear over the other, Belle did her best to compose herself. Kids picked up on things much more acutely than adults and the last thing she wanted was for Connor to get weird vibes from her when she was still figuring this all out herself.

Nick waved to his son and he started for the front door of the vehicle, then saw Belle and clambered into the back seat instead, tossing his stuff on the floor.

"Hey, buddy. How was school?" Nick asked, glancing in the rearview mirror. "You remember Belle, right?"

"Yeah. Hey." The boy busied himself buckling up and rummaging around in his backpack. "Guess what, Dad? I got an A on my science project."

"Awesome!" Nick grinned, glancing over at Belle. "He made a volcano."

"Cool." She turned slightly to peer at Connor. He looked just like a mini version of his dad at the same age. She swallowed the tiny bubble of nervous energy fizzing inside her and forced a smile. "I loved science when I was your age. So did your father."

Connor looked at her speculatively. "He told me you guys used to be friends in school."

"Really?" Belle gave Nick some serious side-eye, her heart beating faster. He'd talked to his son about her? The thought was unexpected and unsettling and a tad bit thrilling. "Yes. We grew up together in Bayside."

"He said you work in some fancy clinic."

"I live in California, near the ocean."

"The movie stars are out there," Nick added, staring straight ahead as he drove back toward downtown. "Belle's a famous plastic surgeon."

"Well, I don't know about the famous part…" she said, watching the scenery again.

Con scrunched his nose. "Are you going to help Analia?"

"Unfortunately, there's not enough time." Belle glanced at Nick again, hoping for some guidance. "But your dad's working on getting her the help she needs."

"Crap." Connor frowned and shifted his weight in his seat.

"Con," Nick said, his tone full of warning. "We don't use that word."

"Sorry." The little boy sat back in his seat again, his expression contemplative. "So, people come to you if they want to look different?"

"Yes, in a nutshell."

"Con's the king of questions," Nick whispered, chuckling low. "He's curious about everything and he's not afraid to ask."

"He seemed so quiet the other day at the funeral," Belle frowned.

"We were both tired and hungry." Nick stopped for another red light and looked over at Belle, his handsome face relaxed as he talked about his son. "Exhausting him is my daily goal."

While Connor continued to chatter away in the back seat and Nick drove on, Belle allowed herself to enjoy the moment and take it all in. Considering this would probably be her last time in Bayside, she wanted to savor it all.

A few minutes later, they pulled up to the curb outside a small restaurant at the far end of Main Street called Piper Cove. She'd not been there since high school, but remembered they had the best chili and hot chocolate in the area. Nick cut the engine then said to Belle, "Hungry?"

Her stomach rumbled and she smiled. "I am."

"Good. Con, time to eat."

"Yum!" The kid scurried out of the back seat to wait with Nick on the sidewalk. A thin coating of fresh snow covered everything, highlighting the impending holidays.

When Belle had been little, Aunt Marlene had gone out of her way to ensure each Christmas was special. They'd bake cookies and watch old movies, even make homemade ornaments for the tree. Now that she was alone, this time of year had lost some of its magic.

Most times she purposely stayed too busy to celebrate. Took extra shifts at the clinic to let the doctors with families have the time off so she didn't sit home alone and feel sad. And, sure, it had been her decision not to turn any of her dates into relationships. Relationships were a luxury she couldn't afford on her pathway to success.

Weren't they?

She got out of the truck and went around to where the guys waited.

As they walked inside the busy restaurant, her conversation with Nick continued to swirl through her head. All this time she'd thought Nick had lied to her, but it turned out he'd been trying to do the right thing.

Belle should've known better. Nick had always had a strong moral compass, even when things were difficult or painful. He'd probably had been right about her too. She wouldn't have been able to live with herself if she'd not kept her promise to her parents back then. Even now, her career still made her feel tied her to them. If she'd stayed with Nick after high school, she probably wouldn't have achieved all she had. That didn't stop her heart breaking for the lovesick kids they'd once been and the lonely people they were now.

"Welcome to Piper Cove," the middle-aged hostess said. "Three tonight? Hey, Connor."

"Hey," Con said, hiking his thumb toward Belle. "This is Dr. Watson. She used to be my dad's friend."

The hostess smiled. "I remember you, Belle, though I doubt you remember me. I'm Mrs. Sweeten. I lived next door to your aunt for a few years. So sad to hear about Marlene."

"Thank you." Belle smiled. "And of course I remember you, Mrs. Sweeten. You used to grow the most beautiful roses."

"Still do," the hostess said, leading them to a table in the corner. "Can I get you all something to drink?"

"Two hot chocolates for us," Nick said, gesturing between himself and Connor.

"Make it three." Belle took off her coat and draped it over the back of the extra chair before sitting across from Nick and Connor. At Nick's raised brow she laughed. "What? I can drink things other than tea."

"Uh-huh. What happened to gluten-free and organic?"

"Hey, I'm entitled to be bad sometimes, right?"

"I do believe we're becoming a bad influence on you, Dr. Watson," Nick said, his little wink sending inappropriate flutters through her insides.

"Perhaps you are, Dr. Marlowe." She picked up her menu, studying it far more closely than was necessary, hoping to avoid doing something silly, like swooning in front of the whole restaurant. She wasn't some teenager anymore. She had an image to uphold. Plus, she'd be gone soon. Best to keep things light and easy, no matter how she might yearn for a real connection. Nick was not the man to help her with that. Not when he was obviously dealing with stuff of his own. She perused the selections, already knowing what she was going to have.

Mrs. Sweeten returned a few moments later with their drinks and took their orders. Three chili and an order of onion rings to split between them all. Not exactly on her list of healthy, low-carb options, but she'd missed the town's home-cooked delights and it was nearly Christmas. If you couldn't splurge at the holidays, when could you?

She took a sip of her hot chocolate, closing her eyes in delight as the warm sweetness hit her taste buds, followed by the rich cream of the whipped topping and the burst of the crushed peppermint topping. The flavors reminded her of all the good times she and Nick had spent here together after school. In fact, the first time she'd kissed him in freshman year had been outside this restaurant, in the little garden to the left of the gift shop. He'd tasted of cherries from his cola and sweet desire.

Belle found herself staring at Nick's mouth now, so firm and full and...

"How'd practice go today, Con?" Nick asked, jarring Belle out of her reverie.

She fiddled with her silverware, doing her best to ignore the heat flowing inside her like honey.

"Okay." Con leaned to the side and waved to someone behind Belle. "My friend Eric's over there by the gift shop. Can I say hi to him? Please?"

"Yes. But be back before the food comes," Nick said, moving his chair forward to let his son get past him. "And no running."

Con hurried away, leaving Belle and Nick alone once more, the confessions they'd made hanging heavily between them like Santa's full sleigh.

"Thank you for telling me about Vicki," Belle said. "It means a lot."

Nick sighed and nodded. "I tend to keep things bottled up these days. It's been hard since she died, with me working so much and trying to do my best for Con."

He looked so forlorn she couldn't help reaching across the table to place her hand over his. His skin felt warm and soft beneath her touch. "I'm sorry."

"It's okay." Nick stared down at her hand covering his before pulling away. "I just... She gave up so much to marry me and I feel like I owe her, you know?"

The guilt in his voice was heartrending. "She wouldn't want you to be miserable, though, would she?"

"I'm not miserable. I'm happy." Nick looked up at

her, his flat tone suggesting the exact opposite. "What's not to be happy about?"

She took another sip of her hot chocolate. She understood his feelings maybe better than most. "Do you remember after my parents died? How I walked around like a robot for weeks?"

"Yeah." His shoulders slumped a bit. "I remember."

"I didn't eat, wouldn't sleep. I was desperate to find a way to bring them back. I thought if I was just good enough, smart enough, I could make them see me from heaven and love me enough to return." She gave a sad snort. "Silly, right?"

"No. Not silly. You were only a kid, Belle. You didn't know any better."

"True." She tapped her fingers against the side of her mug, choosing her words carefully. "But you're thirty-eight, Nick. I doubt Vicki wanted you to live like a monk for the rest of your life."

He blinked at her and she held her breath, hoping she hadn't made things worse. Years had passed, and perhaps she shouldn't say what was on her mind with him like she had back in high school.

"She told me she wanted me to move on, to find someone else. After an appropriate mourning time, of course. She thought it was so funny to tack that on at the end. Vicki had a great sense of humor." He sobered. "But she also had a brilliant career lined up after college. She had her whole life ahead of her. She gave it all up because of one stupid mistake with me." He lowered his head. "I've carried the guilt for a long time, Belle. No matter what I do, I never feel like it's enough. It's a vicious cycle I don't know how to break."

Her heart ached for all he'd been through, for the way he was still torturing himself.

"Hey." She squeezed his hand and ducked to catch his gaze. "Listen to me. I never met your wife, but if she's even half as wonderful as you make her sound then she was a great lady. Smart too. Smart, wonderful women make their own choices. Was your wife a pushover?"

"No." Nick shook his head. "Far from it."

"Then I doubt you forced her to do anything. She chose to be with you and raise Connor. Single women raise children by themselves all the time these days. If she'd really wanted to go off and pursue her career, she could have." Belle sat back. "But she chose to marry you instead."

He watched her closely for a second. "When did you get so wise?"

"I've just learned my lessons over the years. Please stop beating yourself up over something you can't change." She glanced over to where Connor and his friend were playing arcade games. "You've got a wonderful son and a wonderful life here in Bayside. And if the right person comes along, don't be afraid to include them in it."

Nick toyed with his mug, then met her gaze once more. "Physician, heal thyself."

"Exactly."

He narrowed his gaze. "Goes both ways, you know."

"What?" She frowned. "I'm fine."

"Are you?" Nick's too-perceptive stare made her want to fidget. "I know you miss your parents and Marlene, but I hope you still don't think you need to chase after a career you don't love because of some misguided idea you need it to stay close to them."

Her heart lurched. Yes, she'd had her doubts about

the partnership position up for grabs in California, but that was just the usual jitters about the future.

Wasn't it?

Belle sighed and slumped back in her seat. The tiny hollow niggle of discontent in her stomach gnawed harder. She'd worked so hard to get where she was professionally that she'd never taken the time to step back and decide if it's really the place she wanted to be. Honestly, something had felt off inside her from the moment Dr. Reyes had dangled the partnership in front of her like a carrot, but she'd been too busy to contemplate if she wanted to accept. Now, getting out of it could prove more troublesome than it was worth. Especially since she had no idea what she'd do if she didn't take the promotion.

Don't you?

Sweet little Analia's face flashed in her mind again before she shook it off.

No. Giving up a certain partnership for an uncertain future would be ludicrous.

Right?

"Don't be absurd," she scoffed, as much for Nick as for herself. "I'm a grown woman. I've made my decisions based on facts."

"Sure. Uh-huh. Like the fact you made up about me and Vicki during your residency visit?" He took her hand this time and turned it over, rubbing soft circles on her palm with his thumb. "We're friends, Belle. But just in case there were any lingering doubts, your parents loved you and would've been proud of you no matter what. The same with your aunt Marlene. All any of them ever wanted was for you to be happy."

"I am happy," she said, her words emerging about

as convincingly as his had earlier. "I have my patients, my work, a lovely apartment."

"What about friends? Fun?"

"I go out to the movies and walk along the beach and—"

"And here we are, folks," Mrs. Sweeten said, delivering their food.

Belle snatched her hand back, holding it close to her chest as if she'd been burned. She was happy. She had everything she could possibly want.

Except love.

The voice in her head delivering those words was Aunt Marlene's and didn't help in the slightest. She sat back as Mrs. Sweeten placed a steaming bowl of homemade chili in front of her and Nick called Connor back to the table. A platter mounded with onion rings sat in the center of the table. It looked like enough food for six people, let alone the three of them. Then Connor dug into their feast and she realized it might not be enough after all. Nick served up a small plate of onion rings for her and himself then let Con have the rest on the platter.

They ate in silence for a while, Belle savoring her first taste of the delightful chili in almost two decades. So, so good. Thick and hearty, with ground beef and spices and chunks of tomato. And the crispy sweet and salty onion rings were the perfect compliment.

Pure, sinful heaven.

Nick finished first then sipped his cocoa. "The tree lighting ceremony hasn't changed much since you were last here, Belle. There are still vendor booths and crafts plus the community band plays in the bandstand."

"Last year one of the booths had elephant ears as big as your head," Connor said. "Can we get one of those too, Dad? Please?"

"We'll see, son," Nick said. "Finish your dinner first."

She took another bite of chili, her heart squeezing with nostalgia. "Sounds like a lovely evening. Thanks for inviting me along."

"My pleasure," Nick's gaze met hers. "Thanks for accepting."

She'd given him a lot to think about and he'd helped the seeds of doubt within in her germinate too, darn him. The connection they'd always shared flared brighter than ever. It felt as if the years had fallen away. Time seemed to slow, the noise of the restaurant fading until it was just Belle and Nick and the ache in her heart for the way things were, even though she knew it was impossible to go back.

Your parents loved you and would've been proud of you no matter what...

For years, Belle had clung to her one last tie to her parents. It was what had gotten her through med school, residency, finding out Nick had become engaged to someone else. She couldn't abandon it now, could she? No. It wasn't that simple. Couldn't be that simple.

Then Mrs. Sweeten returned to clear their plates and Nick winked at her again, and the world continued on as normal, even as the feeling she'd be losing something precious here in Bayside when she left for good lingered inside Belle.

Half an hour later they walked down the sidewalk on Main Street through the lightly falling snow, Connor and his friend Eric between them. It was night already— darkness fell quickly in the Michigan winter. The streetlights cast a bright orange glow across the glittering ground.

"Wow. The town looks gorgeous all decorated for

Christmas," Belle said, admiring the twinkling lights in a store's window display as they passed. "Beautiful."

"Yeah, it is." Nick drew in a breath and shuffled his feet.

After their unexpected conversation back in the restaurant, he was still trying to wrap his head around the fact he'd bared his soul to her about Vicki. And while the ache of guilt in his chest still lingered, getting things out in the open seemed to have lessened the burden somehow. If he'd taken the time to think about it beforehand, overanalyzing like he usually did, he'd never have brought it up with Belle. Maybe he'd felt comfortable because of her confession in the car about seeing him with Vicki. Man, those words had knocked him for another loop. He'd had no idea she'd visited, or her mistaken assumptions.

A warning claxon clanged in his head, the common-sense portion of his brain warning him that to take this evening as anything more than casual fun between friends would be beyond stupid. And Nick wasn't dumb. Not normally. But having Belle back here again, especially at holiday time, when memories crowded every corner, must have made him sentimental. That's the excuse he was going with anyway.

"Can Eric and I go check out the bandstand, Dad?" Connor asked, nearly bursting at the seams with excitement. "Please?"

"Fine," Nick said, releasing a little bit of his precious control. "But be careful. And look both ways before you cross the street."

Connor and Eric raced on ahead, leaving Nick and Belle to stroll on alone. They each carried a refill cup of hot cocoa from Piper Cove and the sweet strains of "Silent Night" drifted from the concert in the park. As they neared the festivities, things got busier and crowds jostled, all heading to the same destination.

Belle stopped a few times to avoid getting bumped and Nick placed his free hand in the small of her back to guide her safely into Bayside Community Park.

"Wow. This looks the same as I remember." The hint of awe in her voice made him smile. The normally quiet town green was bustling tonight, packed with people awaiting the tree lighting. A huge pine stood in the middle of the square, decorated and waiting for someone to flip the switch. The mayor stood on a small stage in front of the bandstand, trying to entertain the gathered crowds and preparing for her emcee duties.

"Thanks again for inviting me," Belle said, leaning closer so he could hear. Her heat penetrated the wool of his coat and the sweet scent of flowers and soap tickled his nose.

Nick watched her while she looked at the tree, remembering the last time they'd been here together. Their last Christmas before high-school graduation, the night of their trip up to the dunes. That night had been the first time they'd slept together. They'd both been virgins. He wondered if Belle was remembering the evening too.

"Lots of families in the area now, huh?" She glanced up at him before dodging out of the path of a little girl with long blonde hair running straight for them. He slipped his arm around her waist to steady her, then let Belle go when it started to feel too good.

"Yeah. This event always brings the whole community together." He didn't miss the twinge of sadness in her eyes and his own heart tugged in sympathy. Losing Marlene had to be tougher on her than she was letting on, especially at this time of year. A sudden urge to ease that pain welled up inside him, and he shifted his attention to safer territory, the vendor stalls near the side of the park. "They've got cinnamon-sugar roasted almonds. Want some?"

"Yum! Sounds good," she said.

Nick bought a bag for them to share.

"I wonder what color the lights will be this year," he said as they leaned against the brick wall of Gustaffson's World Emporium to watch the ceremonies, the building helping to block the biting wind stirring off Lake Michigan.

Belle smiled. "I think they were purple the first time Aunt Marlene brought me here."

"Then silver." Nick squinted through the crowds, keeping an eye on Connor and Eric near the bandstand. "And red the following year."

"Right. They change them a lot. Who knows what it'll be this year? Maybe all three?"

"Maybe." Nick moved closer to her as more people gathered around them, his heart squeezing with their shared memories.

"Last year they were blue," he said after clearing his throat. A lump of emotion seemed to have gathered there, making his words emerge gruffer than he'd intended. "Connor called it a Smurf tree."

"Nice." Belle laughed and returned her attention to the crowds. The band started a rousing rendition of "Jingle Bells" and people pressed closer as they sang along. Belle linked arms with him so they wouldn't get separated.

Connor and Eric returned, and his son tapped Nick on the elbow. "Dad?"

The countdown to the tree lighting began.

Ten, nine…

Nick was looking at the tree and not his son. "Turn around, Con. They're getting ready to flip the switch."

"Dad!" His son yelled, tapping his arm hard. "Look!"

Nick frowned down at his son. "What?"

"Mistletoe." Connor pointed up above Nick's head.

A quick look skyward had Nick's heart plummeting. Damn. He should've paid more attention when choosing a spot to stand. Belle too glanced upward then met Nick's gaze, a hint of shock and mirth in her emerald eyes.

Eight, seven, six…

"Forget it, Con," Nick said, shaking his head. "Doesn't count when you're just friends."

"Yeah?" his son grumbled. "Then why did you make me kiss old Mrs. Wooten on the cheek at the grocery store? She's not even my friend. She's my teacher. It was yucky."

Belle snorted. "He makes a good point."

"That was different," Nick said, ignoring the heat rising from beneath the collar of his coat. Of all the times and places to have Connor notice the mistletoe, it would have to be now. And Belle wasn't helping at all, standing there chuckling.

Five, four, three…

"C'mon, Dad. It's tradition."

Ugh. The kid wouldn't let it go. Persistence. Another trait he'd inherited from his mom. At the reminder of his wife, Nick waited for the familiar slash of guilt, but for some reason it didn't come. Instead, there was a bitter-sweet sting of longing.

Longing for connection, for peace, for companionship.

On stage, the mayor's hand hovered over the red button to light the tree. Belle bumped into his side, smiling up at him, as radiant as the sun. The same way she'd done their senior year of high school. The same night they'd consummated their relationship. The same night they'd confessed their love…

Two, one…

The crowd gasped as the tree lights flickered on, casting a bright fuchsia glow over the park, but Nick only had eyes for Belle.

"Does kind of seem a shame to waste it, huh?" he said, blood pounding loudly in his ears and adrenaline singing in his veins, drowning out the carolers around them. All his attention was focused on her pink lips, wondering if she tasted as sweet as he remembered.

People swayed around them, pushing him and Belle closer still. Her face was so close, her eyes darkening as their bodies brushed. Their breath mingled, frosting on the chilly air. Time seemed to halt as they seemed to really see each of for the first time after all these years.

Need drove him to take charge. Need and want and years of pent-up denial.

Nick gave up the fight and bent to brush his lips over Belle's.

One quick peck then he'd be done.

People cheered and the band played another Christmas tune, but instead of pulling away, as he'd intended, Nick snuggled Belle closer. She tasted of sugar and cinnamon and chocolate, her body tense against him before she relaxed. Then her free hand was clutching his shoulder and he shivered despite the heat thundering through his bloodstream.

It was as good as he remembered. It was just as right. It was…

Over.

"Hey, Dad?" Connor tugged on his sleeve, forcing

Nick and Belle apart. "Can Eric and I go back up to the bandstand now?"

"Uh..." Dumbfounded, Nick just nodded. His breath was jagged, and he couldn't seem to stop staring at Belle. At her lips, which were still parted. At her eyes, which were wide and looked as shocked as he felt. At her flushed cheeks, which showed he hadn't been the only one affected by their impulsive kiss.

"Yeah," he managed to say finally, turning away to toss the remains of his now-cold hot chocolate in a nearby bin. He took a deep breath and collected himself before facing Belle again. "Sorry. Guess I got carried away."

"Me too," she said, her husky tone sending ripples of awareness through him.

She threw her cup in the trash as well, then crossed her arms, rubbing them against the chill. "We should, um, probably get going. I need to be up early in the morning."

"Right. Sure." Nick called for Connor then started back for his truck, not daring to put his hand on Belle's back again to herd her through the people for fear he might not let her go. His pulse still pounded loudly in his ears and his lips tingled from their kiss. He wasn't sure exactly what had happened between them tonight, only that things had definitely changed.

For better or worse remained to be seen.

CHAPTER SIX

SATURDAY MORNING BELLE was due back at the clinic with Nick bright and early, but she was still feeling slightly off-kilter from their kiss the night before. She wasn't sure exactly what had possessed him to do it, or her to respond, but respond she had. In fact, her insides continued to flutter from the memory of his lips against hers—warm and soft and perfect.

Maybe it had been their conversation in the restaurant. She knew what it was like, carrying around survivor's guilt. She'd done it for years after her parents had died, and it was exhausting. Perhaps Nick had kissed her out of relief after she'd told him it wasn't his fault Vicki had died. Then there was also the fact that last night had been an anniversary of sorts, the night they'd made love for the first time all those years ago, though she doubted he remembered.

No. Last night had been a fluke. A dare started by the stupid mistletoe placed strategically above their heads. No sense getting all nostalgic and sentimental and lovesick about it because she couldn't go there. She had enough on her plate as it was. Belle liked things to be neat and tidy, no messy emotions, no scars. And this resurgence of her connection with Nick was most definitely *not* tidy.

Kissing him last night had been irrational and irresponsible and totally intoxicating and…

Ugh.

Belle pushed through the front door of the clinic, her arms loaded down with donuts and coffee from the bakery down the block and a white plastic bag filled with extra brushes and rollers for their painting job today.

"Hey," Nick greeted her as she walked into the lobby, rushing over to take the box of pastries from her. "You look tired this morning."

"I am. I didn't sleep well last night." She'd tossed and turned, unable to get Nick and his kisses out of her head.

He frowned, his expression concerned. "I hope you're not coming down with something. There's a nasty flu bug going around. My PA said new cases of it are nonstop in my office."

"I'm fine," she said, grateful he'd not brought up the previous evening. Whether he was choosing to ignore it or giving her an easy out, she was good with it. Or she would be, once she got her head on straight. No more stewing about this thing between them. It would all be over soon enough anyway. She only had five more days after this one left in Bayside. A tiny pang of regret pinched her chest before she shoved it aside. It was good. It was all good. And if she just told herself that enough times, maybe she'd begin to believe it. To distract herself, she set the tray of drinks on the counter then took off her coat. "I had my flu vaccination months ago and I'm healthy. Where's Connor?"

"In one of the exam rooms with Eric. I showed them how to use the painter's tape and put them to work blocking off the electrical outlets. Hey, guys?" Nick called down the hallway. "Breakfast is here. Come and get your bear claws before I eat them all."

He turned back to Belle and gave her a guarded smile as Connor and his friend came running, their hair sticking up at odd angles and their matching superhero T-shirts on crooked.

"Good morning," she said, handing each boy a donut wrapped in a napkin. "How are you today, Connor? Eric?"

"Better now that these are here. Thanks." Connor took a huge bite of donut and grabbed a bottled water before tearing back down the hallway.

Eric followed suit, shouting behind him, "Thanks for the bear claw."

"You're welcome," she called after them, laughing. "Looks like the donuts were a success."

"Food's always a big hit with boys. Even big ones like me." Nick took a glazed donut and cup of tea then rested a hip against the receptionist desk while he ate. Her heart flip-flopped. Belle swallowed hard and nibbled on an éclair to hide her flushed cheeks. Nick took a large swig of his tea then held up his cup. "You know, before you came, I was a coffee guy through and through. But you've converted me to your crazy California ways."

She gave a nervous chuckle, looking anywhere but at him. Standing this close to him again, remembering the feel of his lips on hers, the warmth of his breath on her face, his scent surrounding her as he'd held her so close, threatened the careful stability she'd worked so hard to achieve this morning. She needed to stay focused on her goals—get the clinic ready, get the clinic open, get home. Then Nick shifted slightly, his arm brushing her shoulder, and fresh tingles zipped through her nerve endings.

Aw, man. She was in serious trouble.

Not to mention the fact Dr. Reyes had called her

again last night after she'd gotten back to her aunt's house, which was the other reason why she'd not slept well. In addition to the partnership, he'd also offered to let her head up the practice's charity activities. Meaning she'd have free rein and ample resources to put toward the neediest cases. She could travel the world and make a real difference. It was almost too good to pass up, and yet she'd hesitated. Why? She wasn't sure. Perhaps because of the past. Or because of the man in front of her. Whatever the reason, she'd thanked Dr. Reyes and assured him she still planned on being back in California the day after Christmas.

To reinforce the idea to herself, she'd even booked her flight out of Lansing for 5 p.m. on Christmas Day. That should give her plenty of time to run the free clinic with Nick on Christmas Eve, then pack up what was left of her aunt's things before saying goodbye to Bayside for good.

Her heart ached at the thought, but it had to be done.

Amazing as last night had been, it wasn't reality. Reality was that she and Nick had separate lives, separate responsibilities, and Belle wasn't one for flings. So, with her mind firmly made up, she took her tea and her éclair and headed toward the exam rooms they were going to paint. "Best get to work."

"Hey." Nick caught up with her. He lowered his voice and rubbed his hand over the back of his neck, obviously uncomfortable. "About last night…"

"Don't worry," she said, doing her best to sound flippant. "It was just a kiss."

"Right." He narrowed his gaze as he leaned his hand against the wall beside her head. Her breath hitched at his nearness. "Wouldn't happen to have anything to do with your insomnia, would it?"

"No. Don't be ridiculous. We made a mistake standing under the mistletoe and your son called us out on it.
It didn't mean anything." She tossed her hair over her
shoulder and raised her chin, feigning a confidence she
didn't quite feel. "Did it?"

He opened his mouth. Closed it. Looked away, his
frown deepening. "No. I suppose not."

"Good." She sidled around him and headed for the
exam-room door, her heart thudding and her throat dry.
"I'm going to start painting now. Lots to do and little
time."

Thankfully, he didn't follow her this time.

She finished her éclair without really tasting it, hoping the sugar rush would help clear her head and keep
her alert. After finishing her tea, she got busy setting
up to paint the tiny room. Connor and Eric had already taped over all the outlets and Nick had covered
the floors, exam table, and cabinets with tarps. A gal-
lon of beige paint sat on the counter along with a pan,
a roller, and a brush. She'd never really used any of
this stuff before, but it couldn't be hard. After prying
the lid off a paint can and pouring some into a pan, she
picked up the roller and moved the stepladder into position. Starting from the top down would be the most
prudent form of attack.

With her paint pan balanced on the top of the small
ladder, she climbed up and began. The repetitive move-
ments helped soothe away some of her stress and cen-
tered her. She could see why people enjoyed interior
decorating.

"Belle, I think—" Nick walked into the exam room,
startling her.

She turned too quickly and the stepladder wobbled
precariously. Belle squeaked.

Cursing, Nick rushed forward, pulling her close to his chest, his hands on her hips, his muscles rippling beneath the soft cotton of his gray sweatshirt. Molten heat surged through her bloodstream once more, the same kind she'd tried so hard to deny since last night.

"Be careful," he said, voice shaky. "I don't want anything to happen to you too."

Belle saw his face was as white as a sheet, his dark eyes troubled and anxious.

"It's okay." She kept her tone deliberately quiet. "I'm fine. Everything's okay."

Nick let her go and turned away, running a shaky hand through his hair. "Sorry. I'm used to being overly cautious now, since…" Cursing, he rubbed his eyes and forced a stiff smile. "I overreacted. Bad habit these days. After Vicki, I…"

His voice trailed off as he walked back toward the door and her gut wrenched. His normally affable, superman façade faltered. Yep. She'd definitely opened a bubbling cauldron of pain for him last night and now she wasn't sure how to contain it, or if she even should. Aunt Marlene had taught her usually the easiest path to a solution was through the problem. If so, she needed to reassure Nick nothing was going to happen. She rushed forward and placed her hand on his arm. "Hey. Seriously. I'm fine. See?"

"Are you?" Nick looked back at her over his shoulder. "This is all so nuts. I thought I'd dealt with all this stuff already. I'm sorry to bring you into it."

Pretending it's not there won't make it go away. Aunt Marlene's words echoed through Belle's head and she bit her tongue to keep from saying them. Nick was dealing with enough already. Instead, she looked around at the paint now splattering the tarps, ladder and wall.

"Ack! What a mess." *In more ways than one.* Inappropriate laughter bubbled up inside her and before she could stop it, giggles erupted.

"This is not funny, Belle." Nick gave her a stern look before his own lips twitched. Soon he shook his head and started chuckling right along with her. "Okay, yeah, maybe it is a little funny. And definitely a mess."

"I don't even know why it's so hilarious," she wheezed, tears streaming from her eyes. She couldn't remember the last time she'd laughed hard like this and it felt too good to stop.

"Dad, what's going on?" Connor came in with Eric, the two boys looking totally perplexed. When Nick didn't answer right away because he was laughing too hard, Connor rolled his eyes at his friend. "Adults are so weird. Can we have another donut?"

Nick finally collected himself enough to nod then wiped his eyes. "Yes. In fact, bring the box in here. I think we're all going to need extra sugar today. What time are Eric's parents picking you guys up for practice again?"

"Coach said we need to be there by two."

Connor and his friend left, and Belle straightened, attempting to salvage what she could from her pan of paint.

"Listen," Nick said, moving in closer behind her. "I'm sorry about what happened last night at the tree lighting. I don't want things to be weird between us and I had no right to kiss you, okay? It was a mistake and I take full responsibility."

His eager expression was at direct odds with the sharp sting of sadness inside her. She should be happy he regretted their kiss. She didn't want to start anything with him again. She was leaving in less than a week for a glorious new future. So why did it feel like their prom night breakup all over again?

"Apology accepted," Belle said, not looking at him for fear he'd see the hurt in her eyes. Hurt that had no business being there but existed all the same. Darn it. She'd vowed to put Nick and all her feelings for him squarely in her past and now she found herself right back drowning in the emotional deep end with him again. He was right. This was all a huge mistake, but it was too late to get out now. The only way forward for them was through.

She nodded and kept working. "Let's get this cleaned up before the paint dries."

Nick worked for the next few hours, painting alongside Belle, while Connor and Eric played video games in the lobby. Eric's mom picked the boys up around one thirty and he helped Con transfer his gear from their SUV to Eric's mom's station wagon then wished the boys luck before walking back into the clinic. He snorted as he stood in the doorway of the last exam room, pretty sure Belle had almost as much paint on herself as she'd put on the walls, but she was a trouper. Besides, she looked adorable covered in beige.

He stopped short.

Don't go there. You told her the kiss was a mistake. Leave it be.

He should. Nick knew he should. He closed his eyes and pictured Vicki in the hospital. Pictured those last awful days in Atlanta. Pictured Connor waking up crying for his mother in those first terrible nights after his mother had died. Anything to keep him from imagining what it might be like to try again with Belle.

The whole idea was insane. She was only here for a

few more days. Short-term affairs had never been his style. It's why he'd remained alone for two years. Well, that and respect for Vicki. Nick retreated back into the hall and leaned against the wall, taking a deep breath, his final conversation with his deceased wife running through his mind again, as it had so many times the last two years.

I want you to move on, Nick. I don't want you to be alone. Find love again. Be happy. Promise me...

If he concentrated hard enough, he could still smell the sharp astringent odor of disinfectant, could still feel Vicki's frail hand in his as her life had slipped away. He'd promised her he'd be happy, but in his heart he'd vowed to put Connor before all else. Two years later he wondered if Vicki was looking down on him and shaking her head over his lies.

Find love again. Be happy.

It seemed nearly impossible now. It wasn't like love fell from the sky. Not the true kind anyway. Relationships took time and work. Then Belle's off-key humming drifted past his ears and he smiled. They'd loved each other once, but it wouldn't happen this time. She was only here temporarily. Still, the chemistry between them was burning brightly, if the kiss they'd shared was any indication.

Maybe they could enjoy each other while they had a chance. A fling. A brief holiday affair. Maybe he could split his focus between Belle and Connor, if only until after Christmas.

Belle had tried to hide it, but he'd not missed the flash of hurt in her eyes when he'd called last night a mistake.

Perhaps he wasn't the only one who was lonely...

Deep in thought, Nick walked back into the exam

room and picked up his roller to start the final wall. Physically, the work helped ease the tension in his muscles. Mentally, he was a ball of uncertainty, wondering exactly how to bring up pursuing this wildfire attraction between them. It had been so long since he'd dated anyone he wasn't even sure how to start. He turned it over and over in his head so many times, but nothing was certain anymore.

Analyzing every detail made for a great doctor, but not necessarily a great life partner. Vicki had taken a more laid-back approach to things, but Nick and Belle were much more similar personality-wise. Sometimes that was good. Others, not so much. Like now, for instance.

He sighed and ran his roller through the paint again. It was nearly three and they'd worked hard all day. The place looked much better already. Once they finished here and took the tarps down, he'd call the flooring professionals in to do what they could.

Belle's phone buzzed on the counter and she walked over to answer it, wiping her hands on a paint-stained rag. There were splashes of beige on her jeans and in her hair and one streak on her left cheek. He didn't think he'd ever seen a more beautiful sight in his life.

"It's a text from Jeanette. Our supplies will be ready for pick up tomorrow afternoon." She walked over to show him. "I'm done painting my section. Looks pretty good."

"Looks great," he said, straightening to survey the room, then feeling self-conscious as she peered up at him. "I, uh, just need to clean up in here, then you want to grab some dinner? Con's going to spend the night at Eric's after their practice so..."

Smooth, dude. Real smooth.

"Oh." She fiddled with the rag in her hands, twining the cloth between her long, graceful fingers. He couldn't help remembering the feel of those hands on his body, stroking his hair, his neck, his chest, lower still… "Are you sure? I mean, I've got plenty to do at my aunt's house and I wouldn't want you to make another mistake and…"

He took her hand. "I'm sorry, Belle. I shouldn't have said anything. Kissing you wasn't a mistake. In fact, it was pretty great."

"It was?" She blinked up at him and his pulse stumbled. His gaze dropped to her pink lips, reminding him of how she'd felt against him, how she'd tasted. He met her eyes again and saw the same want there that lurked inside him. She recovered quicker than he did, though, her smile brighter than the sun as she bent to help him clean up the supplies. "Sure. Okay. Sounds great. Give me an hour, please. I need to call my office in California and check in on things. Will that work for you?"

Even the reminder of her other life, her other responsibilities didn't dim the joy welling inside him. *Find love again. Be happy.* Just because this was temporary it didn't mean it couldn't be real. He was still mindful of his promise to keep his son a top priority, but surely it wouldn't hurt to take a bit of time for himself this once. "An hour works perfectly. I'll wash my hands and grab our coats and we can head out."

CHAPTER SEVEN

By THE TIME Nick rang her doorbell at around five thirty Belle had showered and changed and was finishing up her phone call with Dr. Reyes. Not exactly a great way to prepare for a date, but then this wasn't a typical date either. In fact, she really shouldn't think of tonight as a date at all. It was dinner and a movie between friends, colleagues. Nothing more. The fact she and Nick had kissed the night before wasn't relevant.

Now, if only she could get her fluttering insides to calm down, things would be fantastic.

She answered the front door and waved Nick inside while still talking to Dr. Reyes on the phone.

"Listen, Belle," her boss said in his usual crisp tone. "I'd like you to give a short speech during the partnership ceremony, perhaps discuss your plans for our new charity work."

"Yes, sir. I can come up with something. Time's a bit tight, though, at the moment. I'll do my best." She motioned for Nick to have a seat on the sofa, trying not to stare at how handsome he looked. He was dressed in a clean pair of jeans, the faded ones that cupped his tight butt and taut thighs to perfection. He'd changed out of his gray sweatshirt from earlier too and now wore a soft-looking black turtleneck sweater topped by his long wool coat and black boots. His hair was slightly damp again from a recent shower and a shadow of stubble darkened his jaw, making him look a bit rough and dangerous. Fresh waves of warmth flooded her core. "Uh, I'm sorry, Dr. Reyes, but I need to go. I'll call again tomorrow to check in, sir."

"Is everything all right, Dr. Watson? You seem a bit distracted," he said.

"Fine. Everything's fine." Her voice sounded strained to her own ears. Distracted was right. And dazed, as Nick grinned, all smooth confidence and lethal male perfection. "Talk to you tomorrow, sir."

She ended the call without waiting for Dr. Reyes's response.

"Patients doing well?" Nick asked as she stood there staring at him. "Are you sure you're not too tired tonight? If so, say the word."

"No, no. I'm good. Sorry." Belle shook off her errant desire to snuggle up on his lap, maybe slide her hands beneath his sweater to feel his warm skin. She took a step back, hoping some extra distance might clear her steamy thoughts. "We should, um, probably get going."

"Yep." His gaze narrowed on her a moment before he pushed to his feet. "Italian food okay with you? I know this great little place just outside Manistee that serves the best baked ziti in the area. Gluten-free, of course. I called and checked."

"Perfect." She smiled and forced herself to move across the room to get her coat from the hook beside the door. Nick stepped in to help her, his warmth surrounding her along with his scent of soap and clean male.

"At first I wasn't sure about this red coat, Belle, but it really suits you." He rested his hands on her shoulders while she buttoned up then turned her to face him. "Are you sure everything's all right?"

"Of course." She pulled on her gloves. "Why wouldn't it be? Let's go."

Forty minutes later, they walked into Casa Antoine's and were seated in a nice banquette for two. After removing their coats, she and Nick perused the menus a maître d' handed them. Belle did her best to concentrate on the food selections and not the man beside her, his thigh pressing against hers, his arm brushing hers occasionally.

"I don't remember this place being here when we were growing up." She took a swallow of water and gazed around at the old-world-style décor. Soft music drifted down from speakers in the ceiling and candles were lit on each table, casting a glow over the room. The place felt romantic and intimate. It only made Belle more aware of the circumstances between her and Nick, the history, the scorching kiss they'd shared. Her hand trembled as she set her water goblet back on the table. Hopefully, Nick was too busy studying the wine list to notice. "You said the baked ziti is good here?"

"The best." He grinned and her knees tingled. "It's fantastic. The house salads are excellent, as well. Do you know what you'd like?"

"I'll try the ziti and a side salad, please."

"Perfect." Nick summoned a waiter over and ordered the same thing for both of them, along with a bottle of cabernet sauvignon. Once they were alone again, Nick fiddled with his silverware, seemingly as nervous as she was despite their kiss, or maybe because of it. "So."

"So." Belle smiled at the sommelier pouring her wine, then waited until the man had finished with

Nick's and left before speaking. "Looks like every-thing's going to plan with the free clinic renovations."

"It does." Nick glanced around at the other patrons. "How's your patient recovering?"

"Good. Good." Belle traced her fingers over the stem of her wine glass, imagining she was trailing them up Nick's chest instead. She swallowed hard against the sudden tightness in her throat. "She's been back for a dressing change and Dr. Reyes says her healing is progressing well. And she's happy, which is the most important thing. How about your meningitis patient?" Belle asked, watching Nick over the rim of her glass as she sipped her wine. "Still improving?"

"Yes. In fact, if she keeps doing well, the hospital plans to discharge her the day after tomorrow."

"Wonderful. She'll get to spend Christmas with her family." Belle sat back as the waiter delivered their salads—finely chopped lettuce and cheese with a light vinaigrette dressing. She took a bite and the tang of fresh greens, garlic and anchovies danced on her tongue. "You were right. This is fantastic."

"Glad you like it," Nick said around a bite of his own salad. "Bread?"

Normally, Belle would've said no, but tonight she couldn't resist the freshly baked yumminess. Her di-etary restrictions weren't because of any health reasons, just that appearances were everything in Beverly Hills. But here with Nick, tonight, she was all about living her life to the fullest. Tonight she'd choose bread and love it too.

After smearing on a healthy dose of the honey but-ter provided, Belle bit into the still warm crusty bread. It tasted so unbelievable that she couldn't contain her groan of pleasure.

Nick paused to watch her, a small smile playing around his lips. "Good?"

"You have no idea."

They ate for a few minutes in silence.

"Is Connor's team any good?" she asked, making small talk.

"Not bad. I mean, they're only eight, so it's not like they're Wayne Gretzky out there or anything." The waiter cleared away their empty salad plates and replaced them with steaming crocks of baked ziti and a fresh basket of bread. Nick thanked the guy then waited for him to leave before continuing. "But, yeah, Connor does pretty well. And he loves the sport, even though I worry about him." At Belle's look, he smiled. "Okay, fine. You were right about that. Those games can get rough sometimes, even in the junior league. But the coach is great, like I said, and takes all the precautions. I'm trying to be better about letting Con have more freedom, like you said. Cut me some slack. I'm working on it."

Warmth spread through Belle over the fact he'd taken her advice, at least a little. "That's great. Connor's a really good kid." She took a bite of the cheesy pasta. "Wow. This is marvelous too."

"See?" Nick grinned. "I wish you'd learn to trust me again."

"I'm working on it," she said, mimicking his words back to him with a grin. And she was too. Belle wanted to rid herself of all her Nick-related hang-ups, but with so little time left she wasn't sure she could open up and let him into her heart once more like she had way back when, no matter how much she might wish she could.

They ate until Belle couldn't force down another bite. She sat back in the booth, feeling full and happy for the first time in recent memory. "Thank you for bringing me here tonight."

"Thanks for accepting." He finished his pasta and wine, then exhaled slowly. "I won't lie. I did have another agenda in asking you here."

"Uh-oh," Belle said, eyeing him warily. "Are you going to seduce me, Dr. Marlowe?"

Belle couldn't quite believe those teasing words had come out of her mouth. Perhaps it was the wine. Or the easy company. Or the fact that for the first time in a really long time she felt at peace and comfortable, without the stress of her job or her future looming over her. Perhaps coming home again hadn't been such a huge mistake after all.

Nick's low chuckle sent a rush of molten heat all the way to her toes. He shook his head, a slight flush staining his tanned cheeks. "Actually, I wanted to talk about our breakup."

Yikes. Talk about a mood-killer.

"Oh." She straightened and fiddled with her napkin again. "It was a long time ago, Nick. I don't really think there's anything left to talk about."

"I feel like I owe you an explanation. Especially after what you told me in the car the other day about coming to see me at Northwestern." He reached over and placed his hand over hers, stilling it. His warm touch was gentle as he rubbed her knuckles with his thumb. "You seem to be under the impression I got over you and moved on a lot quicker than I did."

Belle nodded, staring down at the table. "Okay."

"I didn't." Nick sighed and sat back, pulling her toward him, so their entwined fingers rested in the middle of the table. "I loved you, Belle. You were my first true love. One of the hardest things I've ever done was letting you go back then, even if it was for the best. Afterward, I kept wanting to talk to you, to see if you were doing all right, but you avoided me like the plague. I guess I deserved it after the way I broke your heart, but at least you had your friends and your aunt to talk to. I didn't have anyone."

She frowned at him. "You were the most popular guy in school. What about your friends? Your parents?"

"My parents were both too busy working all the time to have much energy to deal with my teenaged woes. And you'd be surprised how lonely being Mr. Popular can be. Besides, guys don't usually rally around to wallow in feelings the way women do. So I dealt with it like I deal with most things that trouble me. I forged ahead, thinking I'd get over you at some point. By the time I'd gotten to the University of Michigan, I almost believed I'd moved on."

"But you hadn't?" Belle asked, the words scraping a little in her throat on the way out.

"No." Nick shook his head and stared at their joined hands on the table. "I was a mess. I tried dating other people, but it never worked out. I just wasn't into them the way I'd been into you."

"Oh, Nick. What about Vicki?"

"We didn't meet until Northwestern. I was in medical school and she was doing her graduate nursing degree. Nope. U of M was a pretty lonely time for me. I can't tell you how many times I longed to pick up the phone and call you, just to talk and find out about your day."

Her heart ached at the depth of loneliness in his words. "You should have."

"No. I shouldn't." He exhaled slow. "I'd set you free. To call you would have meant my sacrifice was all in vain. You needed to explore your future on your own and I needed to make my own way too. I figured we'd reconnect again if it was right."

Wow. All this time she'd imagined him with a new life without her, happy and content, but it seemed she'd been wrong about that too. So much wasted time.

"Once I met Vicki, we became friends. She was a great listener and gave the best advice. It helped she'd been through a similar breakup. I'm sure she probably got sick of me talking her ear off about you, but she never complained."

"You talked to her about me?" Belle blinked at him, surprised.

"Sure. You're the most important person in my life, and the source of my greatest heartache. Why wouldn't I talk about you? I needed to talk to someone." He shrugged. "Vicki let me get it all out. We bonded. Then one night she asked me to go with her to a party and pretend to be her boyfriend so she could show her ex she was over him. We had a bit too much to drink and one thing led to another…and, well, I've already told you the rest."

His voice trailed off and Belle let her fingers slip free of his. A jumble of emotions wrestled inside her—gratefulness he'd finally shared his side of things, melancholy for what might have been if they'd only reconnected all those years ago, and an odd buzz of adrenaline for the possibilities now during her brief stay in Bayside.

"Wow. I don't know what to say…"

"It's okay. I wanted you to know the truth. Finally." Nick pulled his wallet from his pocket, handing his credit card to the waiter. "Ready to head out?"

She nodded, not trusting her voice at the moment.

"Great." He signed off on the check, then stood and tugged on his coat before helping Belle with hers. "Let's go home."

* * *

The ride back to Bayside was quiet, both of them apparently deep in thought. Or, in Nick's case, feeling a bit hollow after getting all his emotions off his chest at the restaurant. In their wake was a restless energy, pinballing around inside him, making him unsure what to say now. As they took the exit to Business Highway 31 leading into Bayside, Nick glanced over at Belle, trying to gauge her mood. "I enjoyed tonight. Thanks for listening to my rambling."

"Thanks for telling me." Belle looked over at him.

He flipped on the turn signal to make a right onto Hancock Street. "I'm glad we got it all out there. Cleared the air. It was very therapeutic."

Belle snorted. "Gah! Therapeutic? There's a word most people never want to hear on a date."

"Date?" He pulled up at the curb in front of Belle's house and parked his SUV, cutting the engine but keeping the heater running as he grinned over at her through the shadows. Not that he needed any help. Nick was feeling pretty warm already. He unwrapped and shoved one of the mints from the restaurant in his mouth before handing one to Belle too. "Is this a date?"

Belle didn't answer, just ate her mint and stared out the window beside her, making no move to leave. "Dinner was delicious. Back in Beverly Hills I'm usually eating on the run, racing from one procedure to the next. I try to make the healthiest choices."

"Another reason I'm glad I left Atlanta behind." Nick frowned. "Not the healthy choices. The eating on the run."

"Right." She sighed and her smile turned bittersweet. "Well, I guess this is good night."

Belle put her hand on the door handle and Nick

turned slightly to face her, resting one arm atop the steering wheel.

"Wait, Belle," he said, stopping her, his pulse jack-hammering in his ears. It was now or never, and he couldn't remember ever wanting another woman more than he wanted Belle at that moment. Even if it was all temporary. Maybe *because* it was all temporary. "I'd like to keep doing this, with you, for as long as you're here." At her confused look, he said, "Seeing each other, I mean. I'm out of practice with the whole dating thing, but I'm afraid if I don't take the chance now, you'll go running back to California on Christmas Day and I'll regret it."

"I'm not running anywhere, Nick. California is my home." Belle slumped back in her seat and stared straight ahead. "Please don't think I'm not tempted, but we're both dealing with a lot right now. I don't want us to be just another complication. Last night you were mired in guilt over your wife's death and the promise you made to her. What changed?"

"I'm not sure." *Liar.* He knew exactly what had changed. That kiss. He exhaled slowly and stared out the windshield, trying to articulate all the feelings roiling around inside him—apprehension, anticipation, need, nervousness. "I've been living alone for nearly two years now, slogging through my days, thinking it was enough. Then you came back to Bayside and it's like the sun came out again. You made me realize maybe I could do both, be a good father and have a life, at least while you're here. The short duration doesn't make it any less real."

He looked over at her again, hoping his sincerity showed in his eyes. "That's why I think we should have a fling. Explore the sparks we ignited with our kiss.

Take a risk, knowing if it doesn't work out it will all be over soon anyway."

Snow fell softly and Christmas lights twinkled on the neighboring homes. Belle didn't respond and Nick beat himself up internally for making a mess of it all. Vicki was probably shaking her head at him up in heaven.

Tension filled the interior of the SUV like a thick fog. *Way to go, idiot.*

Finally, Belle took a deep breath and squinted down at her hands in her lap. "I found this old embroidered pillow on Aunt Marlene's sofa the other night. It said, 'Bloom where you're planted.' She always used to tell me that growing up. It got me through a lot of hard times."

The pain in her voice stabbed him. Nick scrubbed a hand over his face then faced her again. "I hurt you in the past and I'm sorry. That was never what I wanted. Never. I only ever wanted what was best for you, Belle. I still do."

She gave a little snort. "And you think a fling is what's best?"

"I think we're both lonely and could use a dose of good, old-fashioned intimacy."

His gaze flickered from her eyes to her lips and he leaned in, kissing her slowly and tenderly. She tasted of wine and mint and endless possibilities.

Belle pulled away to look at him, her pupils dilated. "Do you want to come in?"

Nick nodded slowly, his heart feeling too big for his chest. "I do."

CHAPTER EIGHT

BELLE FUMBLED HER keys in the lock, her hands shaking—
not from cold but from nerves and anticipation. She was
doing it. She was taking Nick Marlowe, her old flame,
to bed.

Yes, it would be temporary because she was leaving soon, and quite possibly she was doing it for the
wrong reasons—loneliness, grief, desperation—but
she couldn't seem to make herself care. Neither could
she shake the feeling deep down inside that there was
a good chance this wasn't all wrong. She still cared
for him, far more than was wise. But first they had to
get inside.

She dropped the keys in the snow on the porch.

"Dammit." Belle bent to grab them. "Sorry. This
isn't my usual MO."

"Mine neither." Nick grabbed the keys first and unlocked the front door. "I've got it."

The moment they crossed the threshold he turned
and cupped her face in his hands to kiss her again, more
deeply this time, as if he too needed confirmation this
was really happening. Between the feel of his mouth
on hers, coupled with the memories of how it used to
be, the way they fit—it all seemed a bit like a fantasy.

Then Nick took off his coat and pressed more firmly

against her and she felt his body—hot, hard, ready—
and it became all too real.

This. Was. Happening.

Nick pulled her into the foyer, closed the door then
pushed Belle up against it, his hands sinking into her
hair, tugging gently so her throat was exposed for his
kisses, shoving her scarf aside so his teeth scraped the
sweet spot where her neck met her collarbone. Belle
shuddered with sensation, sliding her hands under his
sweater, to feel the hot skin of his abdomen against
her palms. Her breath caught, tiny, shallow gasps es-
caping as she kissed him back hard, urgency driving
her onward.

They shed the rest of their clothing on the way down
the hall to the bedroom, not caring where it landed,
only caring about this night, this moment, together. So
good, so right, so real.

But by the time they stood beside the mattress, Belle
was nervous again. It had been eighteen years since
they'd been together. They'd both changed. What if he
was disappointed?

Nick sat on the edge of the bed and looked at her,
his brown eyes warm and dark with desire. He took
her hand and kissed the inside of her wrist, meeting
her gaze. Unexpected tears prickled her eyes. This was
Nick, the first man she'd ever loved. The only man she'd
ever loved. Finally, she stopped fighting the craving that
had burned inside her since she'd returned to Bayside.
"I missed you."

He pulled her down and kissed her gently, wiping
away her tears. "I missed you too."

Then his warm hands skimmed her skin, making
her shiver. She leaned into him, nuzzling his neck, her

fingers digging into his strong shoulders. Heat sizzled through her blood like an uncontrolled wildfire.

Belle clung to Nick as he lowered her down beneath him. His solid weight atop her felt like home, at last. She'd never forgotten this. She'd only blocked it out, only tried to pretend she didn't need this. But she did need it, needed him. So much she ached.

He watched her, waiting. "Okay?"

"More than okay," Belle said with a small smile.

His answering grin had joy blossoming in her heart. All those constant worries and warning bells quieted, and she surrendered to this man, this moment. Yes, she'd dated after Nick, but no one else had measured up to this, to him.

She pulled him down for another kiss, their bodies flush.

They couldn't have forever, but they could have tonight.

He licked the pulse point at the base of her neck and chuckled. "Your heart's racing."

"Yours too," she said, pressing her palm to his chest.

His eyes glimmered in the moonlight streaming in through the curtains and he rocked his hips against hers. He was ready. So was she. Belle slid her hand down to caress the length of him. His breath hitched and he cupped her bottom, his face buried in her throat. Her skin tingled from his touch and she arched against him, wanting to be closer, wanting all the space between them to disappear.

Nick got up and quickly put on a condom then rejoined her on the bed. She parted her thighs, letting his weight settle between them. His talented hands seemed to caress her everywhere at once and he took one of her nipples into his warm, wet mouth, suckling her sensitive flesh. Tightness coiled inside her and heat built between her legs. She couldn't wait any longer. She needed him now. Belle reached between them to palm him again, but this time he grabbed her wrist and pinned her hands over her head.

"Sorry," he panted. "It's been too long, and I want you too badly. If you touch me now, it'll all be over. And I don't want this to end."

In response, Belle wrapped her legs around his waist and rocked against him, allowing him to feel how ready she was for him too.

Hanging his head, Nick kissed her and stroked her once more, sliding his fingers down to gently tease her most sensitive flesh. She gasped and pressed harder into his hand. "Yes. Please, Nick. Please."

"Belle," he whispered, his gaze locked with hers as he entered her, stretching and filling her completely. "My Belle."

White-hot desire scorched through her. All that mattered now was this man, this moment, this night. She gave a low, feral groan of satisfaction.

His thrusts began slow and steady, growing stronger and harder as Belle moved with him. Soon passion took over and had them both teetering on the brink of completion. He reached between them once more to stroke her and Belle cried out as she climaxed hard.

After a few more hard, fast thrusts Nick joined her in bliss, his body tight as waves of pleasure washed over him. He buried his face in her hair, whispering words she didn't catch.

Finally, they settled back to earth, his breath warm on her skin, his head resting in the valley between her breasts. She felt weightless and heavy all at the same time, her usual quicksilver thoughts sluggish in the wake of endorphins. Tonight had been as good as she remembered. Maybe even better.

As his breath evened out into the patterns of sleep and her eyes drifted closed, Belle knew tomorrow would bring a return of all the issues between them— their separate careers, his unresolved guilt over his deceased wife, his son and her responsibilities back in Beverly Hills. But tonight it felt like they had their own private bubble, their own private escape from reality.

It was enough. It had to be enough.

Nick awoke before sunrise. Through a gap in the gauzy curtains he saw the snow had finally stopped falling. In the predawn haze he glanced over to find Belle sound asleep on her stomach, her dark auburn lashes fanned on her cheeks and her glorious hair tangled and mussed from his lovemaking. She looked breathtakingly, achingly beautiful.

He waited for the familiar guilt to slam into him hard, but it never came.

Instead, all he felt was tenderness. Tenderness and a tug of nostalgia.

Hard to believe nearly two decades had passed since he'd been with this woman, since he'd let her go and moved on with his life. Yet the connection between them still blazed brightly.

He gently brushed the hair back from her temple. Belle gave a small groan and swatted his hand away, still asleep, rolling over to reveal the creamy stretch of her spine. Unable to resist, Nick kissed the nape of her neck then trailed his lips down her back and inhaled deeply. Flowers and mint and warm, sweet woman. Resting his forehead against her shoulder blade, he did his best to remember every second of their night together, wanting to hold onto it forever.

Belle sighed and he put his arm around her waist, snuggling in behind her again, her soft, plump breast cupped in the palm of his hand. She turned to face him, kissing him before wrapping herself around him. Nick rolled her onto her back and made love to her again.

After they'd floated back from paradise, he kissed her one last time then climbed out of bed, heading for the bathroom and a quick shower before tugging on his jeans. "I don't know about you, but I'm starving."

She leaned up on her elbows, frowning. "Sorry, I don't have much food in the house."

"That's fine." He leaned over to kiss her again, then handed Belle her clothes. "Get up. I've got an idea."

Following a yawn and a stretch, she rushed into the bathroom and closed the door, emerging ten minutes later freshly showered and dressed. She'd braided her damp hair and her green eyes sparkled in the gloom. She looked so happy and beautiful he nearly tumbled her right back into bed again but he stopped himself.

This wasn't real. This would all be over soon. *What about Connor?*

A small twinge of remorse stung his chest before he pushed it away.

His son was fine, tucked away safe and sound at Eric's house.

It was just that it had been so long since Nick had had time to himself he wasn't sure how to handle it. Must be it. He glanced over at Belle and saw her grin. He grinned back. "C'mon."

After bundling up and grabbing his wallet and keys, they headed out to his truck.

Holding her hand, Nick steered with the other

through the deserted streets of Bayside, heading for the bakery downtown, pretty much the only thing open this early. He left the truck running while he ran inside and picked up fresh donuts and tea, then drove to the state park down by the beach. The temperatures were near freezing and their breath crystalized in the air as they climbed the trail to the top of the huge sand dune there, aptly named Old Baldy because of the clearing at the top.

At the summit, he spread out one of the blankets he'd carried up and Belle set out their small feast atop it. Then they huddled beneath a second blanket to await the coming sunrise, just like old times.

The silence between them now felt comfortable as they ate and snuggled while the world around them woke up. From somewhere nearby, an owl hooted. The icy trees crackled in the slight breeze. Everything was quiet and peaceful and pristine in the crisp winter cold.

Nick finished his donut then took a long swig of hot tea and checked his watch. Soon enough, it would be time to pick up Connor. As Christmas Eve approached, things seemed to speed up and the days slipped by so fast. There was still some work to be done on Marlene's old clinic and things to get ready, but all he could think about was spending more time with Belle that didn't involve paint or inventory or work.

His chest squeezed with a sharp pang of warning.

Somewhere inside, a small part of him knew there was a good chance he was using her as a temporary fix for his long-term loneliness, as a way to avoid dealing with his guilt over Vicki once and for all. But he didn't want to think about that now. It had been a long time since he'd been this happy and content and he just wanted it to last a bit longer before reality returned.

He sighed and stared out over the dark, churning waters of Lake Michigan. Being up here again reminded him of their last summer before senior year. Swimming, playing volleyball on the beach, cooking out over a campfire. The first time Nick had realized she was The One had been right here in this spot.

She shifted slightly in his arms and smiled up at him, brushing away a bit of sugar glaze from the corner of his mouth. He kissed her cheek then rested his chin atop her head, her knit hat soft against his skin.

"There's Orion's Belt." Belle pointed at the crooked line of three stars above. "It's the only constellation I know, other than the Big Dipper."

"Me too." He snuggled her closer as she sipped her tea. A thin line of orange brightened the horizon, signaling the impending sunrise.

Belle sighed and leaned away, meeting his gaze as an adorable blush colored her cheeks. "Thanks."

"For what?" The rush of waves against the shore below helped eased the sudden anxiety knotting his gut. It rarely got cold enough for the lake to completely freeze over. Belle shrugged then stared off into the distance. His heart seemed swollen, aching and tender. He tipped her chin up and kissed her again as the sun crested the horizon and the snow shimmered around them. Longing and loneliness pierced him before he pulled back and rested his forehead against hers. "I haven't stayed out all night with a girl for a long time."

Belle chuckled, the sound warming him. "Remember the time we went out on the lake in your dad's boat and fell asleep? We drifted miles up the coast."

"How could I forget?" He smiled and waggled his brows. "You wore a black bikini, the one with the pink flower in the front."

"We stayed up all night then too. It was July Fourth. They shot fireworks out over the water and lit up the sky."

Nick hugged her close once more. "I remember holding you all night."

"Me too." She tucked her head back under his chin for a moment before pulling away. "We should get going before we get frostbite. What time is Connor due home?"

The reminder of his son brought Nick back to earth. "He'll call me when he's ready to be picked up from Eric's."

"Right." She kissed him one last time then pushed to her feet, holding her gloved hand down to help him up. "C'mon. Let's clean up then I'll race you down to the truck. Last one there has to pick up the medical supplies this afternoon."

Belle grabbed their trash while he shook out the blankets then took off after her down the dune. He didn't even try to catch her, knowing he'd be the one heading back to his office that afternoon anyway—to check on his cases and handle some paperwork.

Back to reality, whether he was ready or not.

CHAPTER NINE

BELLE HUMMED TO herself later that day as she restocked gloves and swabs and gauze in each exam room at the clinic. Connor was there helping her, telling her all about his hockey practice earlier and the new video game he and his friend Eric had played the previous evening.

She nodded and smiled when appropriate, though she had no clue about hockey or video games. But it was just as well since her thoughts were still wrapped up in memories of her and Nick together the night before.

In the years she and Nick had been apart she'd been far too focused on her career to consider putting a relationship before her work. Part of it had been ambition, but part of it had been the promise she'd made to her parents, the need to stay close to them. And perhaps another part of it was a tiny secret hope that maybe one day fate would bring her and Nick back together again.

Oh, boy. Don't go there.

"What's this thing?" Connor asked, nose scrunched as he held up a speculum.

"Oh, Um…that's for female exams," she said, shoving the thing back into a drawer below the exam table. "Why don't you fill up the jars on the counter with cotton balls?"

"Sure." Connor grabbed the plastic bag full of white puffs and started stuffing them by the handful into the glass canisters while giving her some serious side-eye. "Do you like my dad?"

Belle froze. Kids were far more perceptive than people gave them credit for, and she shouldn't have been surprised he'd picked up on the connection between her and Nick. Still, knowing what he'd been through with his mother, she certainly wasn't comfortable telling him the truth yet. "Your father and I are friends."

Connor narrowed his gaze. "Like Eric and me?"

"Sort of." Belle fumbled the roll of paper she was putting on the exam table, heat prickling her cheeks.

Connor looked away, shoving more cotton balls into the jar. "My mom died."

Her heart went into freefall and her breath hitched. "I know, honey. I'm so sorry."

"Dad doesn't talk about her anymore." Connor jammed down the cotton balls with more force than necessary. "He thinks if he doesn't talk about Mom, I won't be sad, but it makes me miss her more."

She'd wondered if this conversation might occur and led little boy over to the two chairs along the wall. The fact Nick didn't discuss his wife anymore didn't surprise her. Considering his guilt and his desire to protect his son, it was understandable, if misguided. Still, it wouldn't have helped Connor deal with his loss. Those kinds of wounds didn't heal overnight. She should know. "Tell me about her."

Connor stared down at his toes, his expression bereft. "Like what?"

"I don't know." Belle recalled the things she still remembered most about her own parents, what brought her comfort, things only someone who'd lost a loved one would understand. "What did your mom's favorite perfume smell like? What made her laugh? What was her nickname for you? My mother always smelled like lilacs. And she laughed at cows. Don't ask me why. She's the one who first called me Belle. My dad always called me Chris, but it never stuck the way Belle did."

The little boy sighed, the shoulders of his Blackhawks jersey rising and falling. He looked up at her finally, the sorrow in his eyes squeezing her chest with compassion. "My mom didn't wear perfume. She was allergic. But I always thought she smelled like snow, even in the summer. Crisp and clean. She called me Con, same as Dad. She used to laugh at silly cat videos on the internet. There was one called 'Surprised Kitty' she loved. Want to see it?"

Belle nodded and he pulled out his phone, pulling up an adorable video for her to watch. She couldn't help laughing herself. "Amazing."

"Yeah." Connor gave a sad little smile. "I watch this a lot. Makes me feel better."

"It's good to have things that remind you of her." She put her arm around him, rubbing his arm. "I've found some things at my aunt's house to take back with me to California. Mementos of my parents." She sighed. "I didn't realize how much I missed them until I saw those things again."

Connor blinked up at her. "Must've been hard to lose both your parents. Even though Dad bugs me sometimes, I can't imagine not having him." He stared down at his phone screen. "It's hard, missing people."

"Yes, it is." She pulled the little boy into her side. "But we're lucky, we had people who love us and who took care of us as we healed."

"Dad tries really hard make up for Mom being gone, but sometimes I still talk to her. Weird, huh?"

"No." Belle frowned. "I still talk to my parents too on occasion." She ruffled Connor's hair. "And you should tell your dad this stuff too. Let him know what you're thinking about. You know he's only protective of you because he loves you, right?"

"I guess." He shrugged. "But I'm eight. I can take care of myself." Connor narrowed his gaze on her once more. "If you and my dad are friends, I bet he's bummed you're leaving."

Me too, she wanted to say, but swallowed the words down deep. "He'll be fine."

"My dad's lonely." Connor crossed his arms. "He doesn't think I know, but I do."

She placed her hand on his small shoulder, feeling a warm tug of tenderness. "Your dad's one of the best guys I know. Be patient with him. He's trying." Warm affection swelled inside her for Nick and his son. "Someday you'll both be happy again."

"Really?" Connor scrunched his nose, clearly skeptical.

"Really." Belle laughed. "Thanks for telling me about your mom."

"Thanks for letting me talk about her. I see why my dad likes you so much. Maybe we can be friends too?"

"We can." Her heart felt full to bursting and she blinked back unexpected tears before she stifled them. "We should get back to work before your dad comes in here and sees us slacking. He mentioned something about going for ice cream tomorrow."

"Seriously?" Connor's face lit up.

"Seriously. What's your favorite flavor?"

"Blue moon!" Connor hopped down from his chair

and went back over to the counter to fill a second jar with cotton balls. Belle went back to the exam table, cherishing the fragile bond she'd just forged with Nick's son. Considering she was in her midthirties now, the chances of her having a family of her own were growing slimmer by the year. She'd always thought she'd have children of her own one day. She would've loved to have a little boy like Connor.

"I wish House of Flavors was open in the winter," he said. "I'd kill for a Super Pig."

"Really?" she said, hoping to distract herself from the throb of yearning in her heart. The sundaes he was talking about were huge. Nine scoops of ice cream plus toppings. Nick had eaten a whole one himself once in high school and gotten a badge for his efforts. Belle grinned and finished installing a roll of paper on the table, then grabbed a box of paper gowns to fill the drawer below. "My favorite was the Almond Joy, but your dad always loved—"

"Loved what?" Nick asked, poking his head around the door. "Sounds like you guys are having way too much fun without me."

"We are," Connor said, glancing at Belle. "She and I are friends now too, Dad."

"Great. Belle's an awesome friend." Nick gave Belle an inquiring look as he shrugged out of his coat and slung it over his arm. He winked at her when Connor wasn't looking, and molten warmth spread through her once more. "Don't forget we've got the Chamber of Commerce Holiday Ball later."

"Right." She tucked her hair behind her ear. She'd kind of been hoping to get out of it actually after last night with Nick. It was an annual event in Bayside, lots of townsfolk, lots of dancing and revelry. Lots of gos-

sip over who was doing what and whom. They'd origi-
nally planned on attending to promote the free clinic,
but now Belle would just as soon skip it. Word had already spread about the Christmas Eve reopening and
with what had happened between them last night, everything felt too new and confusing and a bit much, to
be honest. But she had promised the mayor she'd be
there, and she hated to let people down. No. It was too
late to back out now.

She forced a smile and said, "Yep."

As father and son bantered back and forth about Connor's night at Eric's house and the upcoming big hockey
game in Manistee, Belle continued to work and ignored
the sudden sadness welling inside her. She had helped
Aunt Marlene restock these rooms when she was Connor's age. They'd have long talks about life and love and
whatever issues Belle was dealing with. Kind of like the
conversation she'd had with Connor. Up until now, Belle
had done her best to compartmentalize things, keeping her emotions about Bayside away from the situation with Dr. Reyes and her patients back in California.

Now, though, as the last few days in her hometown
drew near and reality sank in, the weight threatened to
crush her like a runaway train. Her crazy schedule had
never bothered Belle before but being back home again
had made her long for a simpler life, for what she'd had
once upon a time here in Bayside.

Thoughts like those were dangerous, though. What
if last night with Nick had been so magical and special and unforgettable because it was fleeting? Rare
things were often the most prized. Long-distance relationships never worked, and Nick hadn't mentioned
wanting one anyway.

He was happy here and she had her place in California.

For eighteen years she'd managed not to get her heart broken again, by Nick or anyone else. And not being heartbroken, not having your life shattered into a million tiny pieces, was way better than the alternative.

Nick pulled up to Belle's house promptly at seven and walked to the front door, adjusting the jacket of his tux with one hand while holding a bouquet of pink roses in the other. He'd remembered they were Belle's favorites, or at least he thought they were. If last night had felt like a date, this evening felt like a test. A test of what life could have been like if they'd both stayed in Bayside and not gone on separate paths. After making love with Belle, they were...

Well, he wasn't quite sure what exactly they were, but the thought of her happy and smiling made wearing a tux again bearable. Con had snorted when he'd taken a look at Nick tonight and shaken his head, telling his dad to say hi to Belle for him. Mollie had looked him up and down and given him a thumbs-up, as well. The residents of Bayside didn't get glammed up often—it was a summer beach town, after all—so the holiday ball was a big occasion. Plus, it would give him another chance to hold Belle in his arms, so Nick couldn't really complain.

He rang the bell then waited, his blood zinging with anticipation.

Belle opened the door, looking amazing. Her auburn hair was twisted atop her head and tiny crystals sparkled from her earlobes. Her long red dress was cut high in the front and low in the back, the fabric falling in a silky rush to her toes. He was pretty sure Vicki had called those necklines halter-style once, but whatever it was named, he was all for it. Eyeing the closure at the back of her neck, it appeared he could give it one tug later when they were alone and remove said gown in a hurry.

Or not. Maybe he'd take his time instead. Nice and slow. Trace his tongue down her creamy flesh, inch by inch, tasting her smooth skin, nipping the spot at the base of her neck that drove her wild, feel her fingers catch in his hair, hear her gasp his name, all breathy and wanton, as his fingers crept up her thigh, taking the dress with them, leaving her fantastic legs bare…

Good Lord. One night with his old flame had turned him into a randy teen again.

"Do I look all right?" she asked, breaking him out of his erotic haze.

"Perfect." He handed her the roses then leaned in for a quick kiss. "Gorgeous."

"You don't think it's too much for Bayside?" she asked, waving him into the foyer while she carried the flowers to the kitchen, putting them into a vase on the table, before she returned to grab her coat and bag. She was wearing the same pumps she'd had on at Marlene's funeral. The slippery, spiky ones that had made her cling to him for support. He was beginning to love those shoes more each day. "I found it in my old closet. I must have bought it to wear to something, but never did."

"No. I would've remembered you in that, Belle. And it's not too much. You look amazing. Every man there tonight will wish he was me." Nick slipped her coat over her shoulders then kissed the nape of her neck, enjoying her slight shiver. "Ready?"

"Yep." She checked her appearance in the mirror once more, then linked arms with him and followed him out to his truck.

* * *

Half an hour later, they were inside the ballroom at the chamber of commerce building on Main Street, a nineteen-twenties architectural gem, filled with intricate parquet floors and art deco décor. The place looked beautiful, filled with poinsettias and white roses and clear twinkling lights. Candles flickered on the tables and wall sconces glowed. They were sharing a table with Jeanette and her husband and Juan and Rosa Hernandez. Nick and Belle took seats across from Jeanette and beside Juan and his wife.

"Hey, Doc." Juan raised his hand. "I'm glad you two are here. I got a call from the plastic surgery office in Detroit today. They want to see Analia after the first of the year to evaluate her for their pro bono program."

"Fantastic!" Nick reached across Belle to shake the man's hand. "Congratulations, my friend. I'm glad all the paperwork we filled out finally paid off."

"We're pretty excited," Juan said. "Haven't told Analia yet. Figured we'd wait until Christmas. She's been praying for this surgery, so it'll be the best present ever."

"Wonderful," Belle said, smiling. "Really great."

Nick squeezed her shoulder, not missing the flicker of disappointment across her lovely face. He frowned slightly and leaned in to whisper, "Everything okay?"

"Fine. Thanks." She waited until the Juan and his wife left the table to dance before continuing. "I just couldn't help picturing myself doing the surgery, even though that's totally impossible. I'm not here long enough to get involved and I'm sure your colleague in Detroit will do an awesome job. Silly, right?"

"No. Not silly at all." He kissed her cheek and pulled her closer into his side for a moment before noticing the scrutiny of his receptionist, Jeanette, from across the table. She watched them closely over the rim of her punch glass, her gaze darting between the two of them before she murmured, "Good for you, boss."

Nick resisted the urge to deny everything, because frankly it was true. Being with Belle these past few days had shown him perhaps there was another way to live, another way to be happy, without his constant burden of guilt. Connor seemed to be adjusting and thriving too, even without Nick's constant hovering. Perhaps his promise to Vicki had been fulfilled. His son was safe and secure. Maybe it was time to stop worrying so much.

"I want you to move on, Nick. I don't want you to be alone."

Vicki's words looped through his head again. A week ago he would've scoffed, unable to picture allowing himself ever falling in love again. But now maybe…

The song ended and Juan and his wife returned just as the salads were being served. Nick sat back, removing his arm from around Belle's shoulders and missing her warmth immediately.

She scooted a bit closer to the table and flicked her napkin open across her lap, picking up her fork and chatting with Juan and Rosa as they ate. "If either of you have any questions about what to expect with Analia's surgery, please feel free to ask. I obviously won't know the specifics but can speak to general things about such cases."

"Perfect," Rosa said. "I actually do have so many questions. What can we expect for our daughter postoperatively?"

"Analia's a lovely girl," Belle said. "But I've not done a full examination so, again, I can only speak in generalities. Be sure to verify all of this with your surgeon in Detroit." She dabbed her mouth with a napkin and took a swallow of chardonnay. "But based on my brief observations of your daughter and my past experience with Crouzon's, I'd say most likely the surgeon with choose to go with what's called a Lefort III procedure. Given Analia's age and the fact she's having issues with sleep apnea, it's the most efficient surgery at this point, though not without complications. It's a long recovery. About eighteen months from start to finish. And it can be challenging."

"What about her eating?" Juan said. "I've done some looking online and belong to a couple of social media support groups."

"Your daughter will need to be on a liquid diet until she graduates to soft foods, so make sure you have straws." Belle sat back as the waiter removed her salad plate and replaced it with the main entrée—roasted chicken breast with veggies. Nick couldn't help thinking how relaxed she seemed, talking shop, and how she'd fit right back into life here in Bayside. For once the idea didn't bother him at all. "Also, be sure she has plenty of clothes she can get in and out of through the front or back, since she won't be able to slip things over her head."

Juan nodded and pulled out his phone to type in notes. "Anything else?"

"You might want to consider counseling, as well."

"Counseling?" Nick stiffened. "Why? Analia's the most well-adjusted child I've ever met. She's always happy. Is a therapist really necessary?"

"Sometimes it helps," Belle said, cutting up her food into small, neat bites. "All of this will be a lot for little Analia to deal with, no matter how excited she is about the surgery. The healing process can be painful. Even the happiest of patients will reach a point of despair before it's all over." She reached over and covered Rosa's hand with hers. "I just want you to be prepared for what you're getting into. It's not easy, but it is worth it, in my experience."

Rosa nodded and Juan put his arm around his wife, tugging her into his side. "We just want our daughter to have a good life. If this surgery makes that possible, then we'll help her through it. That's what families do."

"She's lucky to have you both," Belle said, a hint of sadness in her tone. Nick longed to pull her closer again, but wasn't sure how she'd feel about that, since they'd not really discussed taking this thing between them public. Sure, Jeanette had guessed, but then she spent a lot of time around him. Didn't mean the rest of the town knew. They'd been careful, right?

A string quartet from the local community band began to play again and Nick seized his opportunity. He stood and extended a hand to Belle, bowing slightly. "May I have this dance?"

He didn't miss her slight blush at his request or the sizzle of want inside him it conjured. She took his hand and he led her out onto the dancefloor.

"I'm so happy for Analia," she said. "The surgery will change her life."

"But you wish you could be the one doing it," he murmured against her temple.

"Yes, but as long as you trust this surgeon in Detroit to do a good job, I'm okay with it." She leaned into him, resting her head on his shoulder. "I can't believe I'm saying this, but I'm going to miss this place when I'm gone."

His heart tugged. She hadn't mentioned missing him or Connor, but deep inside he hoped they'd been included in that statement. Swaying gently to the music, he could have stayed there, holding Belle, for an eternity, but unfortunately the song and the moment ended all too soon.

"Ladies and gentlemen, it's time for our annual town service award," the mayor said, taking the stage. Nick and Belle returned to their seats just as dessert was being delivered—a scrumptious gingerbread brandy trifle. "This year we're honoring a very special woman who touched the lives of everyone here in Bayside, Dr. Marlene Watson. And though she's no longer with us, Marlene's spirit lives on in the free clinic which her niece and our own Dr. Nicholas Marlowe will be re-opening for one final time this Christmas Eve. Let's give them both a round of applause for all their hard work during this difficult time."

The mayor waved Nick and Belle up onto the stage to accept a plaque on Marlene's behalf. Once the applause subsided, Nick shook the mayor's hand while Belle stepped up to the mic.

"Thank you all for this. I'm sure my aunt Marlene would've been honored," Belle said, her smile tight with grief. "She loved this town and everyone who lived here. We're honored to grant her final wishes and re-open the clinic for one final hurrah. Please be sure to stop by on Christmas Eve Day starting at eight in the morning until the last patient is seen. No one will be turned away. It's my honor to be back in Bayside and continue to provide the town with the excellent medical care it deserves. Thank you!"

Belle bowed to the crowd then she and Nick headed back to the table. He kept glancing over at her, wondering if she'd realized her parting words made it sound like she might be back in town for good, but she gave no outward sign of it. He shook off the spark of hope inside him. Probably just his wishful thinking.

The quartet started up again and it seemed like the entire town of Bayside was on the dance floor. Everyone was laughing and having a great time and Marlene would've loved it. Afterward Nick placed his hand on Belle's lower back and whispered in her ear, "Want to get out of here?"

"I thought you'd never ask," she said, her voice velvety and low.

They said their goodbyes and Belle gave Juan and Rosa her business card, telling them to call her anytime about Analia. After claiming their coats, he and Belle went out into the crisp December night once more. Thick clouds blocked the moonlight this evening, hinting at more snowy weather moving in.

"Marlene would've loved the ball," Nick said, as he helped Belle across the icy parking lot, his arm around her waist to keep her steady and safe. "You were right. She loved everything about this place."

"Just like you," Belle said, giving him a sidelong glance.

"True." He clicked the button on his key fob to unlock the doors and the SUV's lights flickered. "You too, once upon a time."

"I still do," she said, her head lowered. "More than I should."

"Your speech was nice," he said, wavering about whether to mention it or not, then thinking what the hell. "You should be careful, though. At the end there you almost made it sound like you were staying."

"What?" She gave him a sharp look. "No. I didn't. I just wanted everyone to know we'd give them the best medical care possible, regardless of cost."

"Sure. Okay." Nick didn't miss the way her posture had stiffened or the defensiveness in her tone. He'd obviously touched on a sore spot and didn't want to prod further for fear he'd ruin the amazing thing they had going, no matter how he might want to know what she was thinking.

The drive back to Hancock Street was quiet, with Belle looking out the passenger side window or straight ahead, basically anywhere but at him. Nick knew he'd stepped in it with her and he wanted to apologize, but then they were back at the curb in front of her aunt's house and there was no more time. There never seemed to be enough time for them. He got out and walked around to open her door, escorting Belle up to the house.

"Thank you for answering all the Hernandezes' questions tonight," Nick said while she unlocked the door, debating whether or not to say what was in his heart. Finally, he decided it was better to ask than to regret it forever. "You know, if you did decide to stay—"

Belle sighed. "Please, Nick. Let's not do this right now, okay?" She opened the door and flipped on the lights inside the house. "Want to come in again?"

What he wanted was to continue their discussion, but he didn't want to push her too hard. Not when he could tell she was so close to breaking. So he followed her into the foyer then closed and locked the door behind them before taking Belle into his arms and kissing her gently. This thing they'd started might be messy and complicated and downright impossible, but holding her, kissing her, being with her…felt truer than anything else in his universe.

At last Nick took her hand to lead her down the hall to the bedroom. As he pulled her to him and kissed her once more, undressing her then himself before picking her up and placing her on the bed and stretching out beside her, he reminded himself for the umpteenth time that this was all temporary. Even if it was getting harder and harder to convince himself of that.

CHAPTER TEN

THE NEXT MORNING Belle rolled over in bed, alone, and stared at the ceiling of her bedroom. In the distance she heard the sounds of Nick bumping around in the kitchen.

Despite having him beside her through the night, she'd slept badly. Again. Thanks to thoughts about California and her boss and the new slew of patients waiting for consultations when she got home. A month ago it would've made her happy. Now it just increased the already burgeoning pressure she felt inside. Pressure to do the right thing. Pressure to succeed. Pressure to not let her parents down.

Pressure to make the best decisions for her future.

Being back in her hometown had rekindled her love for this place and its people. It had reopened her eyes to the possibilities of this area and the needs she could fill here. Made her doubt her career trajectory and what she'd thought she'd wanted for herself in the years to come. That might not have been her aunt's intention, but it was true all the same.

She sighed and closed her eyes, whispering a prayer to heaven to please help point her in the right direction. Reality was smacking her hard. Soon this would all be over, and she and Nick would go their separate ways once more.

Pulling away from him at this point would make it less painful.

Now, if she could just get her foolish heart to stop its yearning, she'd be all set.

Belle rubbed her tired eyes and yawned, then forced herself out of bed and into the shower. After scrubbing down and drying off then brushing her teeth, she pulled on clean jeans and an ugly green holiday sweater with a huge reindeer face she'd found in the back of her aunt's closet. It didn't really matter what she wore, since they'd be back in the clinic, making sure all the final touches were in place for the reopening in two days.

Nick was fixing a pot of her favorite tea when she padded down the hall in her stockinged feet.

"Good morning," she grumbled, rubbing her eyes.

"Don't you sound chipper today," he drawled, his tone thick with sarcasm.

"Sorry. Lack of sleep."

"Nothing wrong, I hope."

"No…" She sighed and leaned back against the edge of the kitchen counter. The sound of his voice did things to her—made her think of cozy nights by the fire and sweet kisses and naughty confessions whispered after midnight. Before she could think better of it, she said, "Just thinking about work."

"Uh-oh." He chuckled, making her insides clench and tremble with want. "None of that. Not yet, anyway."

"Are we heading into the clinic again?" she asked, taking a large swallow from the mug of tea he handed her. "I'm ready when you are."

"Stop," Nick said.

"Stop what?" she paused in midsip. "I will fight you for my tea."

"No." He laughed. "I mean let's not go into the clinic today."

"What?" She frowned. "Why? Don't tell me something happened again. We've just replaced all those ceiling tiles and painted and had the floors redone and—"

"No. The clinic's fine. There are only a few minor things left to do and we can take care of them tomorrow. I've got something more fun planned."

The excitement in Nick's tone was contagious and she perked up. "Like what?"

"Come with me and Connor to meet Santa."

"Santa?" She wrinkled her nose. "I think I'm a little old to sit on some man's knee."

"Funny. No, seriously. Con and I went last year, and I think you'll love it. It's on a farm outside town and there'll be shops and live animals and everything. Lots of homemade crafts and food. Come on, Belle. I promise you'll enjoy yourself."

She tried to suppress her smile and failed. It did sound like fun and she didn't have much time left in the area. Might as well enjoy it while she could. "Okay."

"Great. Go put on your boots. No spiky heels," he said. "Even though those shoes of yours give me all sorts of wicked ideas."

"They do, huh?" she grinned widely, the speeding up of her pulse having nothing to do with the caffeine in her tea.

"Oh, yeah. I'll meet you at the door. We'll stop and pick up Con on the way."

Belle went back to the bathroom to put on a bit of lip gloss and smooth her hair back into a ponytail at the nape of her neck, then tugged on her boots. She thought about changing her sweater then decided against it. A festive reindeer with jingle bells on its antlers sounded like perfect Santa-meeting gear. On her way to the front door she pulled on her coat and grabbed her bag before rushing outside. Nick locked the door for her then led her down to his SUV. Hard to believe she'd only been back in Bayside five days. Being with Nick and Connor felt comfortable now, almost like a real family.

Her thoughts snagged on that. No. Not a real family. Only pretend.

She'd be gone the day after tomorrow.

She took a deep breath and climbed into the passenger seat of the vehicle. Twenty minutes later they'd stopped at Nick's and he'd sent the sitter on her way then gotten Connor loaded into the back seat. She flashed the little boy a smile over her shoulder while he buckled his seat belt. "Morning, Con. How are you today?"

He shrugged and looked at his tablet. "Good, I guess. I'm trying to figure out what to ask Santa for this Christmas."

"A very important question." She nodded, glancing over at Nick. "When I was your age, I used to start planning my list in October."

"Oh, I've got stuff," Connor said, frowning down at his screen. "But it feels like I'm missing something."

"I know the feeling," Nick said under his breath, giving Belle a look that had her toes curling inside her hiking boots. "In case I forgot to mention it, you look nice today."

"Thanks. I wore my best Christmas sweater." Belle grinned. "Actually, it's my only Christmas sweater. Another item I found in my aunt's closet." They pulled out of Nick's driveway and she flipped down the sun visor to adjust her hat, settling in for the ride. Snowy hills dotted with cows and horses stretched on as far as the eye could see as they headed out of town. "Doesn't seem as cold today."

"No." Nick glanced in the rearview mirror as a semi passed them, then reached over and took Belle's hand. "It doesn't."

As they drove north, they passed through several small towns. The sun peeked through the overcast sky above, streaming light down on the barren fields. Nick signaled, turning onto a long gravel road. A large sign depicted Santa and his reindeer and read Holiday Farm Ahead. Five Miles. Slow-moving cars rolled along in front of them.

"Ten more minutes and we'll be there," Nick said, glancing at his son in the rearview mirror. "You hungry, Con?"

"Always." the boy said, not looking up from his device.

Nick squeezed Belle's hand, and all felt right with her world, at least for a now. Finally, they reached the large frozen field where attendants were directing people to park. Nick pulled into a slot between two compact cars. "Here we are."

Connor tucked his tablet into the backpack at his feet, his voice excited as he pointed out the window. "Look, Dad. They've got the sleigh again and everything!"

They exited the vehicle and Nick and Belle started toward the ticket booth at the entrance to the farm. Connor raced on ahead of them and Nick slipped his arm around her waist.

"I'm glad you're here today," he said.

"Me too." She nodded, spotting Connor in line for tickets already, nearing the cashier. "We should hurry so I can pay for the admission. My treat this time."

"Belle, I—" Nick started.

"No." She held up her hand, cutting off his protests. "You've paid for all my meals so far. Time for a little reciprocation on my part."

She hurried toward the ticket booth, leaving Nick behind to stare after her.

After buying their admission tickets, they walked through the holiday-themed farm, past brightly lit and decorated trees lining a maze of pathways and vendor booths, displays of fake snowmen and pens with baby animals. The air smelled of hay and livestock mixed with fried food, hot apple cider, and cinnamon.

Inside a large white pole barn was Santa's Workshop, where volunteer elves worked with groups of kids on craft projects—making their own ornaments or wreaths or even small wooden toys. Belle remembered doing something similar with Aunt Marlene one year, shortly after her parents had died. She remembered those hand-made ornaments on her aunt's tree at home.

No. Wait. Not home. Her aunt's house.

Belle's home was in California.

Isn't it?

Crowds jostled past them toward where Santa and Mrs. Claus were stationed near the back of the barn, along with the real reindeer.

"C'mon, Dad!" Connor grabbed Nick's hand and tugged him forward, then did the same with her. "You too, Belle."

She laughed as the boy dragged them inside the pole barn. It was gorgeous and elaborate. Tons more trees, all sparkling in a rainbow of hues. Display after display of animatronic figurines. Ornaments and brightly colored gifts, even a live nativity scene. Above the roar of the crowds, holiday tunes were streaming from speakers overhead, adding to the jolliness. Children and families clustered together, squealing with delight or posing for pictures with the displays.

"The line for Santa's over here," Connor said, pulling on her hand again.

She looked down into the boy's excited gaze and her heart melted. "Did you decide what you're going to ask him for?"

Connor's grin widened, his gaze darting between her and his dad. "Yeah, I think I have."

"Good." She swiveled to look at Nick. "And what about you?"

"I already have everything I need." He leaned in to kiss her sweetly.

"Dad!" Connor scrunched his nose. "There's not even any mistletoe."

Nick pulled away and grinned, his stare amused as Belle's cheeks heated. "Really? I would've sworn I saw some around here somewhere." Then he frowned down at their tickets. "There are specific Santa-visiting times listed on here. We're early for ours. How about we eat first?"

Connor snatched a ticket to verify that then nodded. "Okay. If you're sure."

They walked over to the corner of the barn where tables had been set up near the food stalls. "You two have a seat," Nick said. "I'll get the food. Con, you want a hot dog and fries?"

"Yep," Connor said. "Hey, Dad? Can I run over to the vendor shops really quick? There's something I need to buy. I won't be gone long, I promise."

"I can go with you, if you want," Belle offered.

"No," Connor said fast. "I need to go myself. Please, Dad?"

At first Nick looked like he would say no, but then

he took a deep breath and nodded. "Okay. But only to the vendors, then right back here. I want you at the table by the time the food's ready, yeah?"

"Yeah!" Connor took off. "Thanks, Dad!"

"A hot dog and fries for me too, please," Belle said, taking some money out of her bag to hand to him.

"No, Belle. Keep it. My treat this time." He turned to head for the food line.

Belle sat by herself watching the crowds and thinking how far Nick had come in the past week. She knew what an effort it had taken him to let Connor go off on his own to the vendor booths just now and she was proud of him. Chances were slim anything would happen here in Santa's workshop, but just in case she kept an eye on the shops across the way, spotting the red pom-pom on the top of Connor's hat as he made his way around inside one of the handmade ornament shops, though she couldn't see what he was buying. Probably something for Nick.

A few minutes later, both Marlowe guys were back at the table, safe and sound.

"Here we are." Nick set everything out, including condiments and napkins, then took a seat beside Connor at the table, across from Belle. "Did you get what you needed, son?"

"Yep," the kid said, keeping a protective hand on the small bag he'd carried back.

"Time to see Santa yet?" Connor asked once they had finished their food.

Nick checked his watch. "Still got a half-hour. How about we visit the reindeer now and take some pictures?"

"Cool!" Connor took off down the path ahead of

Nick and Belle. Once they were alone, Nick slipped his fingers through Belle's, warming her chilled skin. An older couple passed them, laughing and snuggling.

"Hello, Dr. Marlowe," the older man said, greeting Nick as they walked by. "Great to see you and Belle back together again."

"Oh, we're not—" Belle started, stiffening, but it was too late. The older couple was already lost in the crowd again.

He did his best to hide the prick of disappointment her denial had caused, even knowing it was silly. He'd known this was all temporary when he'd started this crazy whirlwind affair. This thing between them would end soon. No matter how perfect it might feel to him now.

He squeezed Belle's hand and pulled her into his side as they neared the pens where the reindeer were held. The smell of wet fur and animals was stronger here. Connor's voice echoed from nearby as he talked to one of the reindeer, but all Nick could focus on at the moment was the woman beside him.

They stopped near the corner of one of the enclosures and Nick slid his arms around Belle's waist, turning her to face him. She kept her head lowered and her gaze averted. "Hey, don't worry about what people think. Today's just for fun." He used the same tone he did to soothe his patients through a crisis. "Let's enjoy the time we have left."

He rubbed her back as people wandered past them. Connor was still making his way through the reindeer, petting each snout as he watched Nick and Belle through the fencing.

Gradually, Belle relaxed and Nick pulled back

slightly to brush a few loose strands of hair from her face. "Okay?"

"Okay." She nodded, her cheeks flushing pink. "Sorry. I guess the stress got to me."

"You don't have to carry the weight of the world alone, Belle." He took her chin between his thumb and forefinger. "You helped relieve my burden of guilt over Vicki. Let me repay you now by helping you relax. Ready to see some reindeer?"

Belle gave him a tremulous smile. "Yes. I'd love to."

They joined Connor near a wide pen with the name "Vixen" painted on the wall behind it. The reindeer inside sported a fancy leather collar bedecked with silver bells. Two volunteers stood nearby as the animal nuzzled Connor's hand through the slats, the reindeer's pink tongue reaching for the carrot on his son's palm.

"Dad, take my picture!" Connor called.

Nick pulled out his cell phone and snapped a few photos. When he'd finished, Belle gave him a nudge. "Go over there with him and I'll take a few of the two of you."

Once those were done, Connor piped up again. "I want pics with Belle too."

Nick motioned for her to switch places with him. All of it felt so easy and right. He hated to think about Christmas arriving and this all being over, but he also had to be strong. If not for himself, then for Connor. He'd sworn to keep things in perspective, no strings, no heartbreak. But the more time he spent with Belle the harder his vow was to keep.

"Is it time yet, Dad?" Connor bounced up and down on the heels of his sneakers.

Nick checked the time once more. "Yep. Almost time. Let's get in line."

"Yes!" Connor led them down the fake-frost-covered path. In the distance, Santa's cottage was visible. The sound of a train whistle echoed and through the front entrance to the barn Nick saw a small tractor-pulled locomotive chugging to a stop. He'd read they had one set up around the perimeter of the farm.

Connor noticed it too. "Can we go on the train when we're done?"

"We can," Nick said.

Once they were in line, things moved along fairly quickly. An elf escorted Connor over to a large book on a pedestal and checked whether his name was on the naughty or nice list, then led him toward Santa's cottage. He kept the bag with whatever he'd bought with him the whole time, not allowing anyone else to hold it. While he talked to Santa, Nick and Belle wandered through the vendor booths until Connor emerged from the red and white striped cottage, looking quite pleased with himself.

"Did you tell him everything you wanted?" Belle asked, as they headed back toward the front entrance once more.

"I did," Connor said, walking backward ahead of Nick. "I think it's going to be a great Christmas."

Outside, they took the train around the farm, the snow-covered landscape beautiful, then they stopped for hot cocoa before walking back to the SUV.

"Thanks for today," Belle said, looking over at Nick, her green gaze warm.

"You're welcome," he replied, his words emerging gruffer than he'd intended.

She frowned. "I hope you're not coming down with a cold."

"No, no. I'm good."

"You sure?" Belle tilted her head, watching him closely, her expression concerned.

The fact she was worried about him touched Nick more than he could say. He was used to taking care of everyone else. Having the roles reversed for a change was nice, even if it was only for a short while.

"I'm sure." He leaned over and kissed Belle again. "Let's go back to Bayside."

CHAPTER ELEVEN

THE DAY BEFORE Christmas Eve, Belle was back in the clinic early to scrub down the exam rooms one final time. They were already spotless, but after the supplies had been put away and the front desk readied for patient check-ins, Belle had needed something to keep her from obsessing over the situation with Nick. It seemed like the more she tried not to think about him, the more she did. Their time together was rapidly coming to a close.

Yesterday at the farm had been magical and afterward they'd gone for a nice dinner in town, then Nick had dropped Connor off at home with his sitter so he could rest up for his big game today. Nick and Belle had spent the night together at her house again, but it had been different. The intensity of their lovemaking, the meaning, the poignancy was almost too much, too overwhelming. Especially since they'd say goodbye again in less than forty-eight hours.

She'd been honest with Nick when she'd told him Bayside wasn't her home anymore, no matter how she'd loved revisiting and how much she'd miss the place after she'd gone. She'd built a new life for herself in Beverly Hills, with new opportunities and new responsibilities.

And he had a thriving practice here in town. He

loved Bayside. Neither of them should give up what they'd worked so hard to achieve.

And trying to do the long-distance thing seemed doomed to failure.

Right?

Right. Rock, meet hard place.

After finishing up, she shut off the lights in the exam rooms then wandered down the hall to the reception area. It was quiet here all by herself, but Nick would arrive soon to pick her up. He was handling things in his clinic this morning before taking her to Connor's hockey game in Manistee. She had no idea what she'd be watching, but it would give her more time with her Marlowe guys, so she was happy.

She took a seat behind the reception desk and closed her eyes for what felt like a second. Her lack of sleep was catching up with her, what with the work here to get the clinic reopened, on top of cleaning out all of her aunt's things. Add in the late nights with Nick and her phone calls with Dr. Reyes and she was well and truly exhausted.

"Sleeping on the job?" Nick's deep voice jolted her awake and Belle snapped upright, blinking under the bright fluorescent lights.

"What time is it?" she asked, yawning and squinting at the clock on the wall. "I was resting my eyes and…"

"It's nearly noon. We need to get a move on if we're going to make Con's game on time."

"Oh." She ran a hand over her hair then down the sweatshirt and jeans she'd worn. "Do I look all right?"

"You look perfect, as always." Nick kissed her quick before straightening and handing Belle her coat. "C'mon. Let's get moving."

Thankfully, traffic was lighter today and they made

it to the arena in Manistee with time to spare. They walked inside the cavernous concrete and granite structure and past the ticket booths, up a ramp and into the ice arena. The air was chilly and the shushing sound of skates on ice filled the space. From what Belle could see, both teams were practicing out on the rink on their respective sides before the game. She and Nick took seats near the front row, behind the protective shield of plexiglass, and he helped her off with her coat.

"Where's Connor?" she asked, scanning the names on the backs of the kids' jerseys.

"Over there," Nick said, pointing toward the far side of the rink. "He's playing right defense today."

"Okay." She did her best to get comfortable on the hard, plastic seat and rubbed her icy hands together to generate heat. Connor seemed good at his position from what she'd been able to see in practice, stopping the puck and keeping it from reaching the goaltender behind him. A vendor came by, selling hot chocolates, and she bought one for herself and Nick as the seats around them filled with other parents, including Eric's.

Nick put his arm around Belle again and snuggled her into his side. She was grateful for his heat, though she was still wary of them being seen as a couple. With her returning to California the day after tomorrow, she didn't want to leave him behind to deal with a lot of uncomfortable questions about what had happened. He had too much on his plate as it was. It would be hellish enough to leave. Best to rip the bandage off cleanly, as the old adage went.

She gave him a small smile then pulled away, not missing his frown at her action.

The game began as a referee sailed onto the ice and the national anthem played. They all stood, hand over hearts, to sing the "Star-Spangled Banner." When it was over, she hazarded another glance at Nick and saw those faint lines of tension had returned around his mouth and eyes and her heart sank. She didn't want to hurt him, but this was for the best.

A whistle sounded and the ref dropped the puck and the action increased.

Soon her distress over things with Nick was lost in the cheers of the crowd and rooting for Connor and his team. The kid was good. Even a casual observer like her could tell. Belle vaguely remembered going to Nick's games with Aunt Marlene when they'd been kids, but she'd never really been into sports and hadn't followed that part of his life as much.

"Boo!" Nick stood, shouting as the ref called a penalty against Connor's team. He sat back down, his expression disgusted. "Totally uncalled for. The ref called a body foul on Eric because he bumped into that other kid and tripped him, but it wasn't his fault." Nick cupped his hands around his mouth again. "Bad call!"

Okay. She'd not really seen this side of Nick before, growling and aggressive and alpha, and she had to admit it was kind of a turn-on. Belle grinned and focused on the game once more, doing her best to get into the spirit of things. After Connor's team scored a goal, she jumped to her feet and cheered alongside Nick. "Yay, Connor! Go, Mighty Pucks!"

Nick gave her a side glance, his crooked grin warming her from the inside out.

"You sure you don't want to stick around Bayside?" he asked, laughing. "You make a heck of a cheerleader." He leaned in to kiss her again just as a warning buzzer sounded and everyone on the ice from both teams swarmed to the middle of the rink.

A murmur spread fast through the crowd and Belle looked at Nick. "What's wrong?"

"I'm not sure," he said, scowling. "I wasn't paying attention. Looks like someone's hurt."

Eric's parents were on their feet and heading down onto the ice and it felt like a pit opened up in Belle's stomach as she searched the names on the jerseys, none of them Marlowe. "Where's Con?"

A glance at Nick showed all the color had drained from his face as he stood and raced down onto the ice as well, leaving Belle to follow on his heels. As they pushed closer to the center of the circle of onlookers, the coppery scent of blood filled the air and dread constricted her lungs. Scarlet splotches colored the ice beneath their feet and Belle's pulse kicked into overdrive.

"I'm a doctor, let me through," Nick yelled, shoving parents and coaches aside to reveal Connor flat on his back on the ice, blood gushing from his left wrist as he held it close to his chest and screamed. Nick dropped to his knees beside his son, his voice brittle with shock. "I'm sorry, son. I'm so sorry. What happened?"

Belle pulled out her cell phone to call 911 while one of the coaches fashioned a tourniquet out of gauze.

Nick gently tied it around the gash on Connor's wrist, applying pressure while yelling, "Will someone please tell me what the hell happened to my son?"

"I don't know," Eric said, crying in his mother's arms. "Con covered it right away."

"It was an accident," the coach said, clearly shaken by the amount of blood everywhere. "Con slipped and fell and another kid was right there. The skate blade caught him across the wrist."

After relaying the information and location to the

dispatcher over the phone, Belle moved in beside Nick. "EMS is on the way. What can I do?"

Nick didn't answer, just stared down at his son.

Within minutes, sirens wailed through the arena and two EMTs barreled onto the ice with a gurney, rushing over to where Connor was, in the center of the rink. While one first responder took over the tourniquet from Nick and made an initial assessment, the other talked into the radio mic attached to his collar, sending stats directly to the ER at Manistee General. Once they had Connor stabilized and loaded onto the gurney, one of the EMTs patted Nick on the shoulder. "Don't worry, Doc. We'll take good care of him."

They rushed Connor off the ice and back toward the entrance while Nick ran alongside them, stopping only long enough to toss Belle the keys to his SUV. "I'm riding with my son in the ambulance."

Belle nodded then watched as the group disappeared down the ramp. She quickly ran back to their seats in the arena and grabbed their coats and her bag then hurried to Nick's vehicle, her blood pounding and her heart beating triple time. It was one thing to be the doctor in control, to have emotional distance from the events taking place. It was quite another to have the son of the man she loved in peril.

The ambulance ride to the hospital passed in a blur for Nick.

Dammit. He should've been watching Connor, should've been paying attention. Maybe then he could've warned his son about the impending danger about to strike.

But instead he'd been focused on kissing Belle.

He'd allowed himself to be distracted and everything had gone straight to hell.

I'm sorry, Connor. I'm so sorry.

He'd failed. The final promise he'd made to his dying wife, the woman who'd given up so much for him, and he'd failed her. All for a fling that would be over in days anyway.

No. Belle was more than a fling. Always had been. And damn if that didn't mean he'd let her down too. She'd been up front that what they had was only temporary and Nick had gone ahead and fallen off the deep end for her all over again, heart and soul.

While his world crashed down around him, the EMTs continued to assess Connor's injuries. His son, at least, had stopped crying in agony and now seemed comfortable, an IV of pain meds hooked up to his right arm.

"Can you tell me what you remember happening?" the EMT asked Connor, as he checked his vitals. "Did the blood squirt out or did it ooze?"

Never one to shy away from gore, Connor looked at Nick before answering. "Squirt, I guess. The left winger from the other team was right behind me when I slipped. I hit the ice and his blade went right down my wrist. I covered it as soon as it happened, like my dad taught me."

"Good job, son," Nick said, his words thick, picturing his precious little boy hurt out on the rink. He cleared his throat and blinked hard against the sting in his eyes. This was ridiculous. He was a trained physician. He handled emergency situations with his patients every day. He was supposed to be the calm, rational one. One more area he was screwing up, apparently. He was a horrible father. Familiar guilt descended once more, stealing his breath. This was his fault. He closed his eyes and said a silent prayer. If Connor was okay, he'd do better. He'd not shirk his responsibilities again.

Just please let my son be okay.

They pulled into a bay at Manistee General and Nick waited while the EMTs unloaded the gurney from the back of the ambulance then followed them inside. An ER doc—the same woman who'd handled Nick's meningitis patient days earlier—met them at the entrance in a gown and mask, fully gloved and ready to go. She gave Nick a quick nod of recognition before getting the rundown from the EMTs. Several nurses and techs joined their group as they made their way toward an open trauma bay.

"Sounds like a possible arterial bleed," the ER said as they transferred Connor from the gurney to the hospital bed while Nick stood off to the side. No way was he letting his son out of his sight again, good care or not. "He'll lose blood fast, if that's the case."

"Blood pressure's high," a nurse said, ripping the Velcro of the cuff off Connor's injured arm. "One twenty-six over eighty-four."

Nick's own pulse skyrocketed.

"All right," the ER doc said, smiling down at Connor. "I know it hurts, but I need to take a look at your wrist, okay?"

Connor looked at Nick and he moved in beside the bed, taking his son's right hand. "It's okay, Con. I'm right here with you. I promise."

"Okay." He nodded and tightened his grip on his dad's hand as the ER doc peeled away the bloody gauze from Connor's left wrist. "Ow, ow, ow!"

If Nick could've taken the agony on himself, he would have. Proper punishment for his failures. Instead, all he could do was stand by helplessly and watch as the ER team worked.

"Good, Connor. You're doing great," the doctor encouraged, peering down at the wound. "Can you open up your fingers the whole way?"

His son did as the doctor asked and a bit of the tension constricting Nick's chest unfurled.

"Nice, Connor. Okay." The ER doc looked up at Nick. "He's got good motor function. Good pulses, as well. I'd say we're lucky and it looks like a venous bleed through the muscle only, not arterial. And the tendons look intact, as well."

Nick exhaled his pent-up breath and gave his son what he hoped was a confident smile. "That's good, son. Real good. You're going to be all right."

Connor nodded, the fear in his eyes shifting to relief. "Okay."

"Right." The ER doc straightened as the nurses and techs buzzed around her, checking the monitors hooked up to his son. "What team do you play for?"

"Mighty Pucks."

"I play on the staff soccer team here at the hospital every Sunday. Accidents happen. You try not to get hurt or break anything but, yeah." She glanced at Nick again. "Don't worry, Dr. Marlowe. Once this is healed, your son will be back on his skates and playing as soon as he can hold a hockey stick again."

Nick nodded then allowed one of the nurses to escort him down the hall to the waiting area while they got Connor stitched up. She offered him something to drink, but he declined. The nurse left and he slumped in his seat, wondering how such a great day could go south so fast.

All my fault.

The words continued to loop through his head even though his rational brain knew better. Still, between the guilt and the anxiety and the overall exhaustion of the past two weeks, it was more than he could fight.

He was done. He'd tried opening up with Belle and look where it had gotten him.

She was leaving anyway. Best to end it now so he could focus on his son again.

"There you are," Belle said, running through the automatic doors at the ER entrance and over to his side. "I got here as soon as I could. How's Connor?"

Nick filled her in on the ER doc's findings, his voice robotic, even to his own ears. "They're fixing him up right now."

"I'm so glad. When I saw all the blood on the ice, I suspected an arterial laceration." She took the seat beside his and stared up at the ceiling. "All things considered, you couldn't have asked for a better outcome."

"I can't do this anymore, Belle," he said quietly.

"I'm sorry?" She looked over at him.

"I can't do this anymore." He gestured between them. "Us. I thought I could. I thought I could open up and let myself be with you temporarily, and it would be okay, but it's not. Look what happened to Connor. I let myself get distracted and everything went to hell. I can't allow that to happen again. I'm sorry. This is all my fault. Connor has to be my top priority, now and always."

"Hey." She reached over to take his hand, but he pulled away. "This isn't your fault, Nick. You've been through a shock. Take some time to rest, get Connor home and we can talk later. I'll pick up dinner for you guys and drop it off. Tomorrow we've got the free clinic and—"

"No. I'm sorry, but I'm done." He stood and looked

down at her, his heart breaking even as he knew this was the right thing to do. She had her life and he had his. Trying to mix the two had only led to disaster. "I'll be there for clinic tomorrow, but otherwise it's best if we don't see one another again outside work."

She blinked up at him, as the warmth in her was replaced by sadness. "Um…okay. Sure. Fine. I understand." Belle pushed to her feet as well, avoiding his gaze as she pulled out her cell phone. "I'll just…uh… call a cab to pick me up."

Shit. He'd forgotten she'd driven his SUV here in all the craziness. "No. I'll take you home."

"No, no. You're right. We should be done." Her voice broke a little and part of him died inside. He didn't want to hurt her. Had never meant to hurt her. But it seemed that was their destiny. She sniffled then tapped on her screen. "There. Done. My ride's on its way."

Belle slid the phone back into her bag then glanced up at him, her eyes sparkling with unshed tears. "I'll wait over here. See you in the morning."

He wanted to respond, to tell her to come back, to beg her to stay, but it was all over now. Their fling was done and soon she'd be gone. His life would go back to normal. Just him and Connor and lots of long, lonely nights ahead. He'd get through it because that's what he did.

He wouldn't fail Vicki's memory, or their son, again.

CHAPTER TWELVE

AFTER A SILENT car ride back to Bayside, Belle paid her driver then climbed out to stand on the snowy sidewalk in front of Aunt Marlene's place, watching the glow of the vehicle's taillights disappear around the corner. It was near dusk now and she felt weary to her bones. She slogged inside and flipped on the lights to pull off her soggy boots.

The house was quiet, too quiet, after the hustle and bustle of the hockey game and then the ER. She shouldn't feel so sad, but she did. Nick ending it all this afternoon had been tough, no matter that she should've expected it. With his son getting injured, on top of the guilt still lurking beneath the surface, all of his buttons had definitely been pushed. As a physician well trained in the psychology of her patients, it was a no-brainer. Nick might be a doctor, but when it came to his son's health he'd reverted back to his comfort zone of guilt and Belle had been left out in the cold. Literally.

With a sigh, she padded to the kitchen in her stockinged feet and made a nice cup of tea, hoping it would ease the ache in her chest and soothe the thoughts racing through her mind. At least Connor was okay. Her heart—which should never have been involved in this mess to begin with—was broken, but she'd survive.

She'd suck it up and hide the anguish deep inside, just like she'd done the last time Nick had let her go. Just like she'd done when her parents had died. Just like she was doing with Aunt Marlene passing and the end of her time here in Bayside.

She refused to sit around and feel sorry for herself. She'd keep busy. Lord knew, there was still plenty to get done in her aunt's house before she put it on the market and moved on after Christmas.

Carrying her mug with her, she picked up an empty box in the living room then shuffled to the den to begin packing away the rest of Aunt Marlene's knickknacks. She'd gotten most of the other rooms cleared over the past eight days but had left this one for last. It was the most personal of her aunt's spaces, the one she'd used as her home office and a storehouse for her most treasured mementos.

As she removed each of the framed degrees off the wall with great care, all the repressed sadness and nostalgia inside Belle welled to the surface, despite her wishes, causing her nose to itch and her eyes to sting. She wrapped each frame in tissue paper before tucking the certificate safely in the storage box. Once those were done, next came the local awards for community service, then finally the photos.

Belle couldn't help but smile as she traced her fingers over the pictures. Here was one of her and Aunt Marlene at the county fair shortly after Belle had come to live with her. Another showed her and her aunt at Belle's eighth-grade graduation, a lanky, goofy Nick in the background making bunny ears above Belle's head. Yet another showed a smiling and affectionate Belle and Nick before prom. He'd worn a scarlet bowtie and suspenders with his black tux to match the color of her strapless chiffon dress. Both of them had on their rhinestone king and queen crowns and lovesick, silly grins.

Later that night he'd told Belle he was breaking up with her.

Things between them had been so fun and so magical... until they hadn't been anymore.

Kind of like today.

Dammit.

Her vision blurred and she blinked hard. She wouldn't cry over this. She wouldn't.

She'd gone into this whole affair with her eyes open. It was temporary.

It was over. End of story. Get over it. Move on.

Cursing herself inwardly, she swiped the back of her hand across her damp cheeks and shoved more mementos into the box. She had the clinic to think about in Beverly Hills. She had her successful practice and a promotion waiting for her in California. She was not the same pathetic loser she'd been back in high school the last time Nick had walked away from her, no matter how it might feel now.

Belle pulled their prom picture off the wall and wrapped it tightly in paper before shoving it in the box with the rest of the stuff. Done. She moved on to her aunt's desk. Inside the top drawer were the usual office supplies—pens, paper clips, a stapler, a few rubber bands and a letter opener. She boxed those up too then proceeded to drawer number two.

This one contained duplicate copies of her aunt's ledgers for the clinic. Belle took those out and set them on the desktop. She'd get those to the attorney's office before she left Bayside. They'd fixed up the clinic but given the current real estate market the property would still be a tough sell. Perhaps showing prospective buyers the need for affordable health care in this area would entice their interest.

A glance at the clock showed it was only 8 p.m., but with the lack of sunlight and her exhaustion it felt more like midnight to Belle.

Her heart pinched as she crouched to clear out the final drawer at the bottom. Inside were a few legal pads and an empty scrapbook. Belle pulled them out to put them in the box with the rest of the stuff, then noticed an envelope clipped to the outside of the scrapbook along with another photo of Belle, Nick, and Marlene— this one taken at the clinic. Belle's name was scrawled across the front of the envelope in her aunt's cursive handwriting.

Belle swallowed hard and traced her fingers over the letters, her tears flowing again. Grief over losing her aunt and hurt over ending things with Nick melded with the deeper loss of her parents and her old life here in Bayside. Belle sobbed as she held the envelope to her face and inhaled her aunt's scent—lavender soap and antiseptic. If she closed her eyes, it was almost like Aunt Marlene was in the room with her. She rested her back against the wall and slid down to the floor behind the desk, her fingers trembling as she opened the envelope and pulled out the letter inside. It was dated late October, about a month before her aunt had passed.

Dearest Belle,
Bayside has always been my home and I love it
with all my heart, just as I love you. But if you're
reading this note it means I'm gone. Please don't
mourn for me too long. I had a full and wonder-
ful life with lots of friends and you to keep me
company.

*I'm so proud of all you've accomplished in your
life, just as your parents would have been. You
are my daughter, if not by birth, then by love. You
have more courage and strength and heart than
anyone I know, and you are a true blessing to
your patients and to all of us who love you.*

*But I hope being back in Bayside has reminded
you there's more to life than success and money.
This town is a good place, and there's a real need
for your talents here, Belle. You could make a
good life and a real difference right here in your
hometown.*

*I'm not trying to force you into anything or
make your choices for you, just making sure you
see all your options. Regardless of what you decide for your future, Bayside will always be your
true home.*

Think about it. That's all I ask.
Love always,
Aunt Marlene

After fetching some tissues, Belle sat behind her
aunt's desk for a long time, thinking about everything.
The truth of her aunt's words resonated in her heart.
There was a need here. She'd seen it herself with Analia. She could make a difference, even if she and Nick
weren't together, and honestly that's all she'd ever
wanted. She sighed and lowered her head.

Being here, living in Bayside again would be difficult without Nick, seeing him every day and not being
with him, but she'd cope. The same way she'd coped
with being the new kid on the block in Beverly Hills.
The same way she'd coped with clawing her way to the

top of her profession. The same way she'd coped the first time Nick had said goodbye.

If she stayed in Bayside, she could work out of the old clinic, live here in this house, start a new life from the ashes of her old one. It wasn't perfect, but it felt right.

Still, she wanted to sleep on such a major decision. Considering the day she'd had, waiting until morning made sense.

After a yawn and a stretch, Belle headed for bed.

Nick awoke before dawn on Christmas Eve morning and automatically reached for Belle, before he realized there was only cold mattress beside him. Damn. He covered his eyes with his arm and groaned. All he could picture in his mind was Belle's stricken expression from the day before when he'd told her they were done.

Chances were high he might have overreacted a bit. He sighed and rubbed his eyes.

Okay, a lot.

Idiot.

Opening himself up again to love after years of living in self-imposed denial had been difficult, to say the least. He felt vulnerable and raw and irrational in a way that both thrilled and terrified him. Then yesterday, when he'd seen Connor lying there on the ice, surrounded by blood and crying in agony, every one of his old demons had raced right back to sucker punch him in the gut. He'd immediately closed up, battened down the hatches, circled the wagons. He withdrew, he conquered, he persevered. It's what he'd done after he'd broken up with Belle back in high school. It's what he'd done after Vicki died. And it's what he'd done yesterday.

Such an idiot. A pathetic, gutless idiot.

He lay in the dark and listened to the wind whistle

past the frosty windows. Never mind Belle had been there to support him, that she'd tried to comfort him and point out what had happened to Connor wasn't his fault. Hell, he of all people should've known accidents happened in hockey. He'd played enough of the sport himself and had the scars to prove it. No amount of watching over his son could have prevented what had happened yesterday.

Loneliness threatened to pull him under, but he forced it aside and got up, pulled on a pair of jeans from the day before then padded down the hall to check on Connor. Nick had been up every two hours or so to look in on his son and make sure he was comfortable and not in pain. When he peeked into Con's bedroom, the kid was still snoring away, the white bandages encasing his left wrist glowing in the early morning gloom.

With a sigh, Nick shut the door then went downstairs to start some coffee.

If he was honest, he'd been using his promise to Vicki to push Belle away because he'd been hurting. He didn't want to let her go. Which made no sense, but there it was—he'd pushed her away before she could leave him behind.

Genius. Not.

Yeah, he felt like a real Einstein at the moment. God, he was a doctor. He'd spent more time in school than he'd spent out of it. He was an intelligent guy, a respected part of his small community, yet when it came to his personal life, he was a mess. He tried to put on a brave front, tried to project confidence and control, but in reality he didn't control anything.

Especially the last two weeks.

Belle's image flashed into his mind again—how prim and proper she'd been the night of her aunt's funeral, how she'd gradually loosened up the longer she'd been around him and Connor, how she'd really begun to open up around them. Those thoughts quickly shifted to their kiss at the tree lighting ceremony, the first night they'd made love, the day at Santa's Workshop.

In truth, looking back, the past two weeks hadn't been a mess at all. In fact, they'd been pretty wonderful, because of Belle. She'd made him laugh again, live again, love again, despite his wishes to the contrary.

Find love again. Be happy. Promise me...

Vicki's words returned to his head, making him wince.

Another failure on his part.

Belle had never said the words, but she'd cared about him. Maybe not love, not yet, not on her part anyway, but certainly on his. Then he'd shut her down. Just like last time.

With a groan, he leaned his hips back against the counter as the coffeemaker gurgled away and the rich aroma of fresh brew filled the air. Today was the big day. The free clinic they'd worked so tirelessly to re-open. He should've felt happier about that than he did. Instead he just felt tired. Tired of making the same stupid mistakes over and over. Tired of living like a monk under his self-imposed burden of his guilt. Tired of failing those he loved. How he'd fix things and change his actions in the future, he wasn't sure yet, but, dammit, he was determined to try. He just prayed it wasn't too late. With Connor or with Belle.

She was leaving tomorrow, but there were planes, phones, computers.

Long-distance wasn't ideal, but if she could find a way to forgive him, he'd give her everything he had. He closed his eyes and said a silent prayer.

I'm trying to move on. If I'm doing this right, Vicki, give me a sign. Any sign.

The coffeemaker beeped.

Okay, maybe not the divine choir Nick had been hoping for, but he'd take it.

He poured himself a cup of caffeine then headed back upstairs to shower and change before Connor got up. The clock on his nightstand read six thirty. The clinic was set to open at eight. Mollie would be here soon to stay with his son for the day.

Now he just needed to figure out how to apologize to Belle.

Nick got cleaned up and shaved before dressing in his standard work uniform of black pants, white button-down shirt, blue tie and lab coat. His mind churned and he felt on edge, despite the hot shower. The right words wouldn't come, no matter how he tried to force them. It was frustrating. Today, of all days, he needed to be on his game, needed to be productive and in the flow, needed to have the right thing to say at the right time so Belle would forgive him. There was too much riding on this to mess it up.

After combing his still-damp hair into place, Nick went downstairs to find Connor at the kitchen table, toying with the bandages around his left wrist. Guilt constricted Nick's chest before he shoved it aside. Belle had been right. His son's injury wasn't his fault.

Mollie was in the kitchen, cooking up what smelled like eggs and bacon. She gave Nick a smile as he descended the stairs into the great room. From the open kitchen the sitter waved to him, a spatula in her hand. "Morning, Doc. Looks like you had some excitement yesterday."

"Yeah. Con got a nasty gash on his wrist during his hockey game."

"He told me," Mollie said, unfazed. "Same thing happened to my oldest boy years ago. Live and learn. And watch out for those skate blades."

Nick gave his son a kiss on the top of his tousled head then ruffled his hair. "How are you feeling this morning, kiddo?"

Connor mumbled, giving his dad a sleepy scowl.

"I'm getting ready to go into the clinic," Nick said, walking across the hardwood floor to the fridge. "I wanted to tell you both good morning and I love you, Con."

He swallowed the glass of orange juice he'd poured in one long swallow then set the glass in the sink. After showing Mollie where his son's pain meds were and the instructions from the hospital for changing the bandages, Nick grabbed his coat from the hook beside the door. "Be good, Con."

"Where's Belle?" his son asked.

"At home, probably getting ready for the clinic like I am."

"I don't want her to leave Bayside," Con said, and Nick's heart went into freefall.

Nick sighed and walked back over to the table to take a seat beside his son. "I don't want her to go either, but she's got things waiting for her at home."

"Why can't this be her home?" He jutted out his chin. "Were you mean to her yesterday?"

"No." *Yes.* Nick's chest squeezed, his words sounding hollow even as he said them. "Belle's got a life back in California, son. Don't worry. We'll be fine, no matter what happens."

Connor scowled and crossed his arms. "It's not fine. What about Analia? You're ruining my wish to—" His son covered his mouth before saying any more, his eyes wide.

"Analia's got an appointment with a doctor in Detroit after the holidays." Nick's thoughts ran back over the last few days and his gaze narrowed with suspicion. "Wait. Is that what you asked Santa for? To have Belle stay and operate on your friend?"

"No." His son picked at the pine tabletop. "And fine isn't fine at all. Nobody's happy."

Nick sighed and glanced at the clock then stood. This conversation was going nowhere fast. "Look, I'm sorry, Con. Sometimes there are no easy answers, but I really have to go or I'll be late."

"Whatever." Con waved him off and put his head down on the table.

Talk about feeling like the world's worst father.

As Nick drove to the clinic, he did his best not to dwell on the argument with his son and instead focused on finding the right words to say to Belle.

I'm sorry. I'm an idiot. I'm in love with you and I don't want to lose you again.

As he sat at a red light, Nick's stomach knotted. Today really wasn't the day to blurt out his feelings to Belle, but if not now, then when? She was leaving Bayside tomorrow, most likely never to return. The light turned green and he drove on slowly through the slick streets, still snow covered from the night before.

Uncertainty twisted tight knots in the muscles of his upper back between his shoulder blades. He'd been playing it safe for two years since Vicki's death, not causing any waves that might bring up painful memories for Connor and trying to control the world. But now Nick wanted more. He wanted Belle by his side, through good times and bad. To see her face first thing in the morning and last thing at night. He wanted to plan for a future for the three of them together, as a family. He was not prepared to say goodbye again.

But the only way to get to the future he wanted was to deal with the present. To talk to Belle today and find out what she wanted.

He pulled onto Main Street and spotted a line already forming in front of the clinic. Old people, young people, kids, infants. Nick parked his truck in the employee lot behind the building and huddled in his coat as he headed toward the back entrance. All the lights were on inside, meaning Belle was already there. Anticipation and apprehension tingled in his gut.

He walked inside and took a deep breath, catching the scent of antiseptic and fresh paint. The low hum from the heating vents in the ceiling and the buzz of the fluorescent lights filled his ears. Beyond them were the sounds of Belle tinkering around in the lobby. He took off his wool coat and straightened his lab jacket then headed up front, spotting Belle behind the registration desk. According to his watch, they had about half an hour before the doors opened.

"Hey," he said quietly, when she glanced over at him. "Can we talk?"

Before Belle could respond, Jeanette arrived to take over the front desk. Disappointment bit deep. He didn't want to have a difficult conversation with Belle in front of his office manager. Dammit. Heat prickled up from beneath the collar of his starched white shirt as faces pressed to the glass doors at the entrance and patients jostled to get inside out of the cold. Normally, before a long day in the office, he liked to take a few moments to center himself, get his head in the right space, but today he felt completely discombobulated.

Maybe it was better to dive right in and deal with work first.

Then he and Belle could talk later, after they closed.

That would give him more time to consider his actions too. The rational part of him was still insistent that ending things with Belle had been the right thing, even if his timing had been questionable. Perhaps instead of apologizing and begging her to stay, he should instead make sure she understood this was all for the best. After all, his guilt and need for control were his issues to deal with, not hers. Until he made things right within himself, he shouldn't bring her into it. She had a whole life waiting for her in California. He'd never ask her to leave her career and her dreams behind. He'd been through the same with Vicki and had learned his lesson. He didn't want to live with regrets anymore. Even if his heart felt shattered into a million pieces.

CHAPTER THIRTEEN

BELLE'S DAY HAD started two hours earlier with a phone call to Beverly Hills. It had been the middle of the night there, but Dr. Reyes had still been in the office. A cautionary tale of workaholism she was grateful she wouldn't be repeating. He'd picked up on the second ring, and Belle had squared her shoulders, preparing for the difficult conversation.

"On your way home already?" Dr. Reyes had said by way of greeting. "I knew you'd be anxious to get home to civilization."

"I am home, Dr. Reyes."

"Back in California? Perfect. I'll send a driver to pick you up and bring you down to the office. There are a few things we need to go over on the new cases you'll be taking on after the partnership is finalized."

"No, sir." Belle had taken a deep breath. "I've decided I'm staying in Bayside."

"Excuse me?" His surprised tone had quickly turned to anger. "Don't be ridiculous, Belle. You're tired. Get on a plane and get back to Beverly Hills. I need you here."

"Perhaps, but there are people in this area who need me more." She'd sighed and rubbed her eyes. "I'm sorry, Dr. Reyes, but I can make a real difference in Bayside."

Analia's face had flashed into her mind and the more she'd talked, the more confident she'd felt about her decision. "You know my ultimate goal was always to help people. I feel the best place for me to do that is right here in this area. There's a great need for medical resources and I believe I can do more to help others here in Bayside. Therefore, I'm resigning from the practice effective immediately. I'll continue to follow up with my current patients remotely until their cases are concluded, as per my original contract, but once those are closed, I'm done. Thank you for the opportunity, but I'm just not happy there anymore."

He'd continued to sputter but she'd ended the call and put the phone down.

One difficult situation concluded. Today was the second. They had the free clinic to run, which meant working side by side with Nick. But deep inside her sense of inner peace had returned. She'd made the right choice, no matter how things with Nick turned out.

When she'd gotten in to the clinic this morning, the first thing she'd done had been to call Juan Hernandez. He'd been surprised too, thinking something else had gone wrong at the clinic. But when she'd asked him to come in today, along with his wife and daughter, Belle had felt an excitement bubble up inside her she hadn't felt since med school.

Signal two she was on the right track.

The minute Nick walked into the clinic, Belle's skin prickled with awareness and her chest pinched with yearning. She longed to tell him about her conversation with Dr. Reyes and her decision to stay in Bayside, but then she remembered his words from the day before.

It's best if we don't see each other again outside work...

Work. Right. That's what she was here to do. That was why she was staying.

She hazarded a quick glance at him over her shoulder as she went through the appointment book again with Jeanette and her heart skipped a beat at his handsomeness. Even in his work clothes he was still the most gorgeous man she'd ever seen. Nick would find out soon enough about her change in plans anyway. She'd need to buy out his half of the clinic in order to use it for her new plastic surgery practice.

"How's Connor this morning?" she asked, looking away again.

"Good. Slept through the night," Nick said, his tone gruffer than usual. "He's on the mend. Look, Belle, I—"

An older lady with a cane outside rapped on the glass, pointing at her watch.

"We should probably get started," Belle said, ignoring the rush of nerves inside her. Not nerves over seeing patients but over what Nick had been about to say. She didn't need any more drama right now, good or bad. "I'll go unlock the doors. Everyone ready?"

Jeanette nodded. So did Nick, though his expression looked as conflicted as she felt.

The minute she had the doors unlocked, the older lady with the cane limped in and headed straight for Jeanette. "Twyla Phillips. I need a refill on my diabetes meds pronto. With the weather, I haven't been able to get in to see my doctor in Lansing and now they're closed for the holidays."

"Sure, Mrs. Phillips," Jeanette said, handing the older lady a clipboard. "Just have a seat over there and fill out these forms and we'll be happy to help you."

Twyla toddled off to the chairs against the windows

and Jeanette began slowing working her way through the line of people coming in.

Belle went back into one of the exam rooms to wait for the first patient to complete their paperwork and make their way down the hall. As she was fiddling with the instruments laid out on the counter—tongue depressors, cotton swabs, an otoscope, a reflex hammer—she heard the sound of a wet, hacking cough echo from the hall, followed by Nick's calm, professional tone.

"I'm glad you came in to see us today, Mr. Banks," Nick said, leading the patient into the exam room across the hall from hers. "Regular checks of your CHF are important. Can you tell me what meds you're currently on?"

Nick glanced up and caught Belle's gaze as he started to close the door. The warmth in his brown eyes hit her first, followed by the instant sizzle of connection that was always there between them, whether they wanted it or not. Her lips parted and her breath caught and she nearly ran across the hall to beg him to let her back inside his life again, but then the moment passed as Nick shut his door and Belle's first patient appeared.

"Doctor?" Twyla Phillips said, limping into the room and handing Belle the papers in her hand. "I need help with my diabetes meds."

"Sure thing." Belle's professional persona slipped firmly back into place. "Have a seat on the exam table for me and we'll see how we can help you today."

After going over Mrs. Phillips's vitals and medical history, Belle wrote her out a two-week prescription for her insulin to get her through the holidays then sent her on her way. Next came Mrs. Welkins and her grandson, who was also her caretaker. Her dementia had progressed far enough that she didn't verbalize much and she was quite thin, but really the only problem she had was a need for more of her medication.

The patients became a bit of a blur after that. There was John d'Andre, who suffered from morbid obesity and diabetes and had also developed a small ulcer as a result of poor circulation. He got a certificate for some free antacid, courtesy of Bayside's local drug store, and a referral to a gastroenterologist in Manistee. Then there was Mr. Whitlaw, the father of one Belle's elementary school classmates, who'd sliced his finger open making breakfast. Belle gave him three neat stitches and sent him on his way.

Between visits, she ran into Nick in the hallway as she took her files back up to Jeanette, but other than a murmured "Excuse me" as they passed each other, they didn't have a chance to talk at all. Even lunch was rushed, consisting of a quickly consumed half of a sandwich in the back storeroom between cases. It was hectic and crazy, and Belle loved every minute of it.

It only reinforced to her she'd made the right choice to stay in Bayside.

Even if Nick didn't want to see her anymore.

Finally, around five that afternoon the crowd of patients began to ebb. Belle was finishing up with a little boy with food allergies who'd developed a rash after eating some Chinese food. She'd been explaining to the mother how her son should take the medications she'd prescribed him when there was a knock on the exam-room door followed by Jeanette poking her head inside.

"The Hernandez family are here to see you, Dr. Watson."

"Great." Belle walked her patients up to the reception desk and greeted Juan and his wife before crouching before Analia. "Hello, pretty girl."

"Hi." Analia grinned, her dark eyes sparkling with energy.

"You wanted to talk to us, Doc?" Rosa asked.

"Yep. C'mon back to the exam room and I'll fill you in." Belle led them down the hall and gestured for the trio to enter before her then followed them inside. She was just about to close the door when Nick opened his door across the hall. Their gazes met, his eyes flickering to the Hernandezes behind her before returning to Belle.

"Is there a problem with Analia?" he asked, his expression concerned. "She's my patient. Perhaps I should take her case."

"Hey, Doc," Juan called out, raising his hand in greeting to Nick.

"There's nothing wrong with Analia," Belle said, swallowing hard. He'd find out soon enough anyway and though this wasn't the ideal situation to tell him about her plans, it worked as well as any considering how busy their day had been. She took a deep breath and raised her chin. "Nothing I can't fix anyway. I've decided to stay in Bayside and open my own plastic surgery practice here. I wanted to speak to Analia and her parents about the possibility of me taking over the surgery for her Crouzon's."

For a moment all Nick could do was stare down at her.

Belle was staying.

Part of him wanted to whoop and holler. The other part of him, the analytical part, wanted to ask her why, wanted to know what had brought her decision about, wanted to know if she planned to live in her aunt's house and work out of this very clinic.

"If you'd like to sit in on my consultation with them, as Analia's pediatrician, that would be most helpful," Belle said. "You obviously know them better than I do and might put their minds at ease."

He opened his mouth to respond. He'd love nothing more than to work on a case with Belle, to work on building a life together too, but before he could say a word, Jeanette hurried down the hall toward them.

"Sorry to interrupt, but Bayside PD just pulled up out front. Seems one of their officers was injured in the line of duty."

Nick snapped his attention from Belle to Jeanette. "How bad?"

"Not sure, but they brought him here first since it was the only clinic open in town today." Jeanette headed back up front as the bell over the front entrance jangled.

Damn. "Sorry." Nick winced. "I should see what's up."

He started to back away as Belle nodded. "No problem. I'll fill you in later."

She walked into the exam room and closed the door behind her and for the first time since before Connor's accident, hope flooded Nick's system. Belle was staying. She was staying and he'd have another chance with her. One he did not intend to miss.

But first he had another patient to treat.

The once crowded lobby was empty now as closing time rapidly approached. Blue lights from the squad car parked at the curb flashed intermittently through the frosted front windows of the clinic. Nick walked over to help the female officer get her injured comrade inside.

"What happened?" he asked, as they maneuvered the hurt cop into an empty exam room. The man was middle-aged and doubled over, holding his right side.

Nick didn't see any blood or signs of trauma, but he couldn't rule out anything serious just yet. Bayside was hardly a hotbed of violent crime, but there was the occasional gunshot wound from a hunting accident.

"We stopped to help a motorist with a flat tire out on Highway 31 and my partner slipped on the ice and fell on his shoulder," the female cop said. "He only had surgery on it last year."

"Okay." Relief spread through Nick. A possible torn rotator cuff was much easier to handle. He and the other cop got the guy into the exam room and up on the table. The injured officer scooted around awkwardly, apparently unable to use his right arm. "You're going to be all right, Officer...?"

"Mowbray," the injured cop said, his voice strained, his face pale. "Stupid of me. My wife told me to wear my good boots today, but did I listen? Nope."

Nick scribbled down the man's account of what had happened in the file. "Don't worry, Officer Mowbray, I'm going to take good care of you." He set the file aside and moved in to examine the man's shoulder and arm more closely. "Can you slide out of your jacket and shirt for me so I can see the extent of bruising?"

The officer did as he asked and Nick palpated the man's shoulder joint, noting the white scars crisscrossing the area from the aforementioned surgery. Gently he tested for range of motion and extension of the patient's arm then checked the officer's blood pressure on his uninjured arm before allowing him to put his shirt back on.

"Okay. Well, the good news is I don't think it's broken or another tear. The bad news is you should have an X-ray to be sure and we don't have a machine here.

You'll need to go up to Manistee General to have it done. Sorry."

He stepped over to the counter and pulled out his cell phone, making a quick call to the hospital to see if they could fit the officer in. After getting the okay from the tech, Nick returned to his patient. "Right. The hospital says if you can get there within an hour, they'll fit you right in. Otherwise it could be awhile, with the holiday rush and all."

"I'll make sure he gets there," the female officer said. "Safely this time."

"I'm fine, Ethel. Stop fussing," Officer Mowbray said, waving off his partner. "You're worse than my wife."

Nick grinned, pulling out a sling from the cabinet and fitting it over the officer's right arm before turning back to the counter to write out two scripts, one for an NSAID pain reliever and the other to put the man off work pending the results of his X-ray and a consult with his orthopedic surgeon. He turned back to Officer Mowbray and handed him the papers. "The tech has instructions to call me with the results when they're done. Even if everything's okay, you'll most likely still end up with a nasty bruise. Take it easy until you hear back from me. Got it?"

"Got it," Officer Mowbray said, letting his partner help him down from the exam table. "Thanks for this. Merry Christmas to me, huh?"

"Yeah," Nick snorted, opening the exam-room door for them. "Merry Christmas indeed."

He glanced over to find the exam room Belle had been working in with the Hernandez family dark and empty. Damn. He checked his watch and realized he'd been in with the cops longer than he'd anticipated. Following them up to the reception desk, he glanced at the clock on the wall. Five forty-five.

"Drive carefully," he said to the officers as they exited. "Happy Holidays."

"Same to you, Doc," Officer Mowbray said, raising his good hand at Nick. "And Happy New Year too."

Once they'd gone, Nick turned to his office manager. "Where's Belle?"

"She left about five minutes before you finished," Jeanette said, walking over to lock up the clinic door and flip off the lights. They were officially done. "Said she had some things she needed to take care of before Christmas."

Nick's first instinct was to go after her, track her down and beg her forgiveness.

But first he needed to get Connor. Mollie had family coming to stay with her for Christmas and she needed to get home. He tossed Officer Mowbray's paperwork on the desk, then took off for the back of the clinic. "Thanks for your help today, Jeanette. I'll come back and clean this place up later. Right now I need to get going. Can you lock up behind you?"

"Sure thing, boss," Jeanette called from behind him. "Merry Christmas!"

"Merry Christmas," he yelled back, as he grabbed his coat and headed for his SUV. If he could get to Belle and convince her to give him another chance, it would be a very happy holiday indeed.

CHAPTER FOURTEEN

THE BAYSIDE TOWN green looked even more magical to Belle than it had the night of the tree lighting ceremony. The huge tree glowed from the center of the space, shades of pink and silver and white glimmering off the newly fallen snow on the ground. Carols were piped in from speakers attached to the nearby buildings and the area was nearly deserted as people spent the day with family and friends. Belle strolled through the winter wonderland, enjoying the peace and quiet after the controlled chaos of the clinic all day.

Home. She was finally home. It had taken her eighteen years and reuniting with one complicated, compassionate, completely wonderful doc and his son to make her realize this was where she belonged, and now she was here, she wasn't leaving again for a long, long time.

Well, if you didn't count the drive up to Manistee for little Analia's surgery.

She couldn't help smiling when she recalled the conversation with the Hernandez family back at the clinic. They'd barely let her finish explaining her plans to stay in Bayside before they'd accepted her offer to take on Analia's case free of charge to them for the chance to do the difficult but necessary surgery. There'd still be bills from the hospital, of course, but the donation of her services would help immensely. And perhaps Manistee General and the other doctors and technicians involved would get on the bandwagon, as well. Analia was such a special case and she seemed to charm everyone around her.

Belle walked around the tree then took a seat on one of the ornate wrought-iron benches toward the back of the area. Hopefully, Nick's last case with the police officer went well. After she'd finished with the Hernandez family, he'd still been in the exam room with his patient, so she'd gotten the rundown from Jeanette. No blood, so perhaps a fight or a fall. Whatever the injury, she prayed it wasn't life-threatening and the officer would be home with his family for Christmas.

Then she'd come out here to collect her thoughts before talking with Nick again.

She blinked up at the dark sky, icy flakes melting on her cheeks. "Thank you, Aunt Marlene. Thank you for bringing me back to Bayside. Thank you for giving me another chance with Nick."

Even if he doesn't want to be more than colleagues.

Belle sighed and stared down at her red-mitten-covered hands in her lap. Soon she'd have to head back to the clinic and face the man she loved, explain her reasons for staying here in Bayside. She wanted nothing more than for him to sweep her off her feet and proclaim his undying love and whisk her off to happily-ever-after. Except this wasn't some fairy tale, and she was hardly a princess in an ivory tower. She was a world-class plastic surgeon and a force to be reckoned with, both in and out of the operating room. She'd be fine, with or without Nick.

Her heart squeezed.

But things would be so much better with him. Him and Connor.

The sound of a car door slamming resonated through the small park, followed by a voice.

A very familiar voice.

"Belle?" Nick called. "Dr. Christabelle Watson, where are you? I saw your rental car at the curb. I know you're here somewhere. You can't hide from me forever."

You could make a good life and a real difference right here in your hometown...

"Thanks again, Aunt Marlene," Belle whispered, then stood. Her breath hitched and her legs shook as she moved around the enormous tree to see her Marlowe guys waiting for her on the other side. Hope shimmered between them like tinsel. "Hey."

"Hey." Nick moved closer. "Jeanette said you left for the night."

"I did." She smiled down at Connor. "How's your wrist today?"

"Better, thanks." The little boy squinted up at her. "My dad says you're not leaving."

"True." Belle crouched to be closer to his eye level. She noticed he had the bag from Santa's Workshop in his hand. "I'm going to stay in Bayside and work here from now on."

"Will you operate on my friend Analia?" Excitement flared brightly in the little boy's eyes, so like his father's. "Help make her normal?"

"I will. And Analia is already normal. I'm just going to make her outside better reflect the beautiful girl she is inside. I spoke to her family about it an hour ago." She grinned at Connor then looked up at Nick. "As long as it's acceptable to her pediatrician, of course."

"Of course." Nick held out his hand to her as she straightened. "Thank you."

"No." She squeezed his gloved fingers with hers, tears stinging her eyes. "Thank you. Thanks for letting me be a part of your family and your life these past two weeks. Thanks for reminding me of what I loved about Bayside and why this place still feels like home even after all these years away. Thanks for showing me I can make a real difference here." She sniffled and shook her head, lowering her gaze. "I know you've got things you're dealing with and you don't want another relationship, and I respect that. But I hope we can at least be good friends and colleagues."

He tipped her chin up, forcing her to meet his gaze. The lights from the tree cast them in a rosy pink glow and the tune on the speakers switched to Aunt Marlene's favorite carol. It all seemed too good to be true, and yet the heat of Nick's leather-covered thumb stroking her jaw told her it was real. It was also better than a fairy tale because they'd both weathered the storms of life and survived. They'd survive the future too. Together.

"I want to apologize for the things I said yesterday at the ice rink. I overreacted and I'm sorry. I saw Con hurt and in pain and let my emotions take over." He looked away, shaking his head. "I'm a doctor. I should have known better, done better. I've been trained to be cool, calm, rational in trauma situations, but I lost it yesterday and that's all on me. Can you forgive me?"

She pulled his hand from her jaw closer to her chest, over her heart. "There's nothing to forgive. Your son was in pain and injured. You acted like a father, not a physician, which is exactly what you should've done. We're good."

"We are?"

"Yes." Belle nodded, doing her best to keep the flare of apprehension welling inside her from bubbling over and failing miserably. "And you're sure you're okay with me working on Analia's case? I know you put a lot of time into setting things up in Detroit and—"

He stopped her with a finger over her lips. "I'm good with it. In fact, I'm thrilled. It will make things a lot easier for Analia and her parents to be close to home during the whole process. Plus, it will save them money in the long run." He smiled, his warm gaze igniting a wildfire inside her. "I'd love to observe and consult as needed, if you'll let me."

"I wouldn't have it any other way, Dr. Marlowe." She turned her face slightly to smile. "We're still partners, remember?"

Heat sparked in his eyes as he leaned in to kiss her. "Always."

Nick's lips brushed hers, softly, gently, before capturing her mouth and deepening the kiss. The hesitation inside her vanished and the tiny ball of tension in her core unfurled. This was right. This was good. This was perfect. This was…

The clearing of a throat broke them apart.

"Dad," Connor said, staring up at them. "No mistletoe again."

"I'm sure we can find some around here," Nick said, grinning, his arms still around Belle's waist, holding her close, his heat warming her from the inside out. "And you'd better get used to it, son. I'll be kissing her a lot in the future, if she'll let me."

"She will," Belle said, laughing. "Are you finally going to show us what's in the bag, Connor?"

"Well, it is Christmas Eve, so…" He pulled out a small wrapped gift and handed it to Belle. "Here."

Pulling free from Nick, she sat on the bench to open it. "For me?"

"Yep." Connor bounced on the toes of his snow boots. "Picked it out the day we went to the Santa Farm."

She carefully unwrapped the tiny box to find a pink crystal heart inside. Engraved on the front were all three of their names.

Belle looked from Connor to Nick then back again. Nick took a seat beside her on the bench and wrapped an arm around her shoulders, pulling her into his side. Her voice shook as she said to Nick, "Did you know about this?"

"Nope." He put his arm around his son and pulled the little boy into his other side, hugging him tight. "But considering the weird trajectory of our relationship so far, why should our proposal be any different, eh?"

"Our proposal?" Belle asked, glancing back and forth between father and son.

"Yep." Connor grinned at his dad. "We talked about it on the way over here. We want you to come live with us forever, Belle. We promise to love you always, even when my dad acts like kind of a doofus."

"Con," Nick warned.

The little boy just shrugged. "So, Belle. Will you marry us?"

Her vision blurred with tears as she lifted the delicate object from its tissue paper nest and nodded. "It's beautiful."

"You're beautiful." Nick leaned his forehead against hers. "Is that a yes?"

She kissed Nick sweetly then reached over to carefully hug Connor as well, mindful of his injured wrist. She couldn't have wished for anything more. A true home. A new family, not just for Christmas but forever. A second chance to build the life she'd always wanted. "Definitely a yes. Merry Christmas, Nick. Merry Christmas, Connor."

"Merry Christmas, Belle," Nick kissed her sweetly on one cheek while Connor did the same on the other. "I love you. Always have, always will."

"Me too," she said, cupping Nick's cheek then kissing the top of Connor's head. "I love you both too."

* * * * *

LET'S TALK
Romance

For exclusive extracts, competitions
and special offers, find us online:

- facebook.com/millsandboon
- @millsandboonuk
- @millsandboon

Or get in touch on 0844 844 1351*

For all the latest titles coming soon,
visit millsandboon.co.uk/nextmonth